The Method
and Other Stories

To Tish

with my very best

Tom S V[illegible]

The Method
and Other Stories

TOM
VOWLER

CAMBRIDGE

PUBLISHED BY SALT PUBLISHING
14a High Street, Fulbourn, Cambridge CB21 5DH United Kingdom

Printed in the UK by the MPG Books Group

Typeset in Bembo 12 / 13.5

ISBN 978 1 84471 804 7 paperback

1 3 5 7 9 8 6 4 2

for Alison

Contents

The Method

I'D READ ABOUT those actors, the purists who immersed themselves in roles for months, sometimes years, collecting all the experiences, the essence of characters in order to portray them better. If they wanted insight into how being the middleweight champion of the world felt, they'd seek it in the ring from the end of someone's fists.

My own approach to research had never been this committed; if I wanted to write about something, I'd read about it. I'd Google the hell out of it and then use my imagination to make notes and diagrams, charts with lines linking characters, the complex worlds they occupied, their beliefs, histories, idiosyncrasies, what I thought they ate, how they voted. I'd construct their lives, give them voices, breathe life into them. I thought that was enough. But then, at a meeting with my publisher, the issue of authenticity arose.

'I'm not sure we believe in Will,' said Gillian.

'In what way do you not believe in him?'

'He doesn't seem . . . organic.'

'He's not a root vegetable.'

'The voice slips at times and I'm not really sure what he's feeling when he, you know . . .'

'Sleeps with large women?'

'Yes. Why do they need to be so big?'

'It's a childhood thing.'

'And the drug-taking sections . . . they sound contrived.'

'What do you suggest?'

'We like the novel per se. Joff was raving about its filmic potential.'

'I'm not really . . .'

'We do need to airbrush this . . . what's he called?'

'Will.'

'Yes. He doesn't resonate. Parts of him feel made up.'

'They are.'

'Yes, yes of course. It doesn't feel as if you know him well enough. Is he essential?'

'To what?

'The story.'

'It's called "Will's Island".'

'Yes, I wanted to talk to you about the title.'

Once home I got out my notes on Will. Five-eight, early forties, loss adjuster turned journalist turned would-be novelist. I conjured the image of him into my mind, walked around my office talking like him—actual lines of dialogue from the early chapters. I sat down and sketched his face, pinning it above my monitor next to the list of onomatopoeic verbs I made one grey Tuesday afternoon. I began a conversation with him in the mirror, introduced him to Rapunzel, whom he meets in Chapter 14 anyway before her violent end sixteen pages later. I liked him.

I emailed Gillian: WILL STAYS.

As Will had done, I typed 'dating large women' into Google, and as Will did, I signed up for three of the sites. I looked at some profiles but none of their creators looked big enough. Will's thing, you see, is losing himself, almost literally, in women. Their arms and legs, their breasts, have to engulf him. He lets them crush him like he were a written-off car.

Elaine, 37, from Bath, looked the largest of them, so I emailed her. Two weeks and three dates later I was beneath her lolling stomach as it slapped hard onto mine like a trawler landing its catch.

'Can you just lie on me, really still?' I said, which is what he gets them to do.

'Oh, Will,' she moaned.

Diane, 39, from Exeter, had bigger thighs and arms, but said I wasn't her type. I told her she wasn't mine either and that it didn't matter. She didn't finish her drink. A couple more objected to me talking into my dictaphone as they came. Furthermore, none of them matched for mass those I'd described in the latter chapters. There were sites dedicated to bigger women, but their purpose was merely two-dimensional; there was no scope to meet them. Others implied a financial exchange, but as Will doesn't do this, I was reluctant to. Instead I considered the relativity of size.

In the meantime, I turned my mind to other parts of his life. Will had worked on a national, but I had to start somewhere. The editor at the *Herald* explained that their trainee journalists were usually straight from college, an English or media degree behind them, some post-grad study to boot. But he'd heard of one of my novels—the one they dramatised badly—and said to go in for a chat.

'Bit late for a career move, isn't it?'

'I think reporting's in my bones.'

'Might be a bit dry for you: council meetings, petty crime . . .'

'Dry's good.'

'Send some articles in and we'll see.'

My largely embellished CV meant I had to learn quickly. Sleeping three or four hours a night, I studied contempt of court and local authorities and was up to seventy words a minute shorthand in a fortnight. I spent two whole days in the library reading every piece in every *Herald* from the last five years. There was such a depressingly formulaic structure that I wondered how Will had coped with it. Three weeks after meeting the editor, I walked around the town interviewing its dreary cohorts as they went about their newsworthy business. I sent in three disparate stories and a week later I was a trainee journalist on twelve grand.

If I couldn't make the women bigger . . .

Calories became my nemesis; I could tell you how many were found in almost any food. I cut down to six hundred a day, then four hundred. I jogged to and from work and used the paper's gym in my 'lunch' hour. I hadn't exercised since my twenties and my body let me know it. Initially, the changing room was the only place I drew attention.

'Shit, mate. You lose any more weight, you'll be able to fax yourself to work.'

I got breakfast down to an apple. Lunch was a banana, dinner a tin of tuna.

I grew a beard; reading my notes and the early chapters again, I found no reference to Will's, beyond that he had one. His clothes were easier to mimic, though I needed ever smaller ones.

Now there was less of me, I joined some more sites.

'Shit,' said Caroline, 42, from Clevedon, as I took off my shirt. 'Your spine, I can see all along it.'

I told her I had cancer and was on one final pilgrimage of fornication.

'I must be three times your weight.'

'More, I hope.'

The mention of illness backfired, got her thinking about STDs, so in the end I went for honesty.

'I need to know what it feels like,' I said.

She wouldn't have sex but was solicitous enough to roll about naked on top of me, my frail body barely able to support her.

I emailed Gillian the new chapters.

Editors are like headmasters, I discovered, in that they call you in to their office a lot.

'Are you sure you're not having a breakdown? Change of career. Change of name.'

'I've just never liked David.'

'So we're to call you Will, now?'

'Will Reed.'

'Have you looked in the mirror lately?'

'Is that a song lyric?'

'I'm sorry, David —'

'Will.'

'It's just not working out. You can see the week out in the newsroom—you can't interview people looking like that.'

This was fine. It took me ahead a few chapters—to where Will loses his job—before I'd had sex with a colleague, but I sought insight rather than replication. However, I was still eager to recreate Chapter 8's strong denouement. I walked to my desk, lifted the monitor up in order to throw it through the window. My mistake was obvious. In my description I had it detaching from the other hardware easily, before ending up in the car park two floors below. In reality, the cables held it in place like guy ropes and so I placed it back down, Gillian's voice in my head waxing indignant about verisimilitude. I settled for shoving everything to the floor and made a mental note to revise the scene.

After being fired, Will descends into recreational drugs. He figures it's essential to embarking on a creative path. Literature, he decides, should be born of a reckless devotion to euphoria and its pursuit. Everything from rapture to depravity must be tasted and experienced in all its splendour and misery—sort of a bank of sensations to withdraw from when needed.

He scores off a stranger in the pub—a nod, a wink and to the gent's for a furtive exchange—but after a fruitless night in the town's less salubrious establishments, I knew this would also have to be rewritten. In the end, a friend of a friend gave me her friend's number and told me to text for a rendezvous.

Will's language as he gets stoned came easily enough from personal experience, but my descriptions of his cocaine and heroin consumption were, shamefully, Googled for. (Chat rooms and blogs with exchanges of narcotic experiences are ubiquitous, with users comparing highs and comedowns; I'd simply amalgamated a few.)

The gram of coke in my inside pocket made me feel like a mischievous schoolboy all the way home in the taxi. I began with a few small lines over an hour or so, editing the relevant chapter as I observed myself. If anything, I'd overstated the language, for there was no obvious intoxication, no clear transition from straight to high. I just felt a warmth, a sense of near bliss. As I wrote, everything was lucid and beyond the need for revision. I typed the keys like a concert pianist, yielding sublime, mesmeric prose. This wasn't work, it was my essence expressing itself. Will was almost certainly one of the great characters in literature. I snorted some more, stayed up working on the manuscript until dawn before sleeping lightly for a few hours. A profuse lethargy held me for most of the next day, but otherwise I felt fine.

I knew heroin was going to be different.

The shoplifting was easier than I thought, making me wonder why I had ever paid for anything. The trick appeared to be in your body language: maintaining a sanguine, guilt-free posture whilst smiling effusively at staff as you left the shop usually sufficed. Only once did I have to sprint away, pursued by a tenacious but fortunately rotund store detective.

Tattoos, though, hurt more than the hot scratch I'd described. The man inflicting the pain told me I'd chosen a particularly sensitive area for such a skinny person. I told him Will had chosen it to impress a woman, which left him looking unimpressed.

My dealer was unsurprised to see me back so soon, but thought my progression along the chemical spectrum a little alacritous.

'You go easy with this, my friend,' he said.

In my ignorance I had assumed Will injected, and as I tied the tourniquet above my elbow and searched for a willing vein, I began to wish he'd smoked or snorted it. The sienna powder had been reluctant to dissolve, so I'd added a few drops of lemon juice, which renders it PH neutral, a trick Will didn't know about. After heating the underside of the spoon, I could draw the liquid into the syringe. I then flicked the barrel and expelled any air. I eased the needle's bevelled tip into a vein at forty-five degrees and pulled back the plunger a little, bringing up a small plume of puce into the brown. I removed the tourniquet with my teeth, pressed the plunger home and lay back.

The next day, when I'd finished being sick, I emailed Gillian the new version.

Spending a night in a cell didn't concern me unduly; what Will did to get there did. I had never hit anyone before, let alone been struck myself beyond scraps at school. I'd asked my estranged brother to punch me, but he'd just returned from a retreat and said it would unbalance his chi. Me hitting him was also out of the question.

Will argues with some men across a pool table before a fight starts — a lazy cliché, now that I read it back. In the Mermaid I challenged the winner to a game and he obliged. As he cued I appraised his shot selection with derisive *tuts*, I took an age when it was my turn and then denied fouling a ball, but they seemed to allow men with pin heads for pupils and pin cushions for arms a certain dispensation. They even offered to buy me a drink and someone handed me a leaflet about rehab.

The Cow and Plough looked more promising. It had no pool table, but several men were sat alone on stools with a do-not-disturb posture. The first was listing badly and barely registered my diatribe. Further along I found a more willing research assistant.

'You only hate them,' I said, 'because deep down you wonder what it's like to have a cock inside you.'

Despite inviting the punch, it still surprised me. There was none of the *whip crack* you hear in films, no *kapow* or *phwack* from cartoon bubbles. Just a silent jolt, a sickening judder as my head swam about. I clamoured for adjectives, checked the sensations. And then I launched myself at him. No technique, no grace, just limbs whirling out of pure hatred. Few connected, and I took some more strikes, but the adrenaline flushing through me was rivalling the stuff I'd snorted and stuffed into my veins.

The next morning the duty solicitor came into my cell to advise me they were going to charge me with common assault.

'It needs to be ABH,' I rasped through a distended top lip.

The heroin was doing two things: assisting my weight loss further whilst ensuring no woman would look upon me as reasonable sexual material. The fight had also given my face several new shades and claimed three teeth. And anyway, conventional seduction was now beyond me.

My advert, although sounding extreme as I typed it, felt tepid once it was posted among the others on the website. I set a lower limit of twenty stones, alluded to what I'd be prepared to pay, logged off and gorged myself on Bach whilst shooting up.

As I slumped back on the sofa, I could just make out the answer-phone kicking in and Gillian's voice: *Hi David. Love the new chapters. So visceral. So real. Call me. Ciao.*

There were no scales in the house, but as I stood in front of the bedroom mirror I reckoned I'd lost half my body weight. Ribs protruded from my concave chest; I could almost push a finger in behind them. My legs were barely broader than the bone. Skin stretched across my sinews and joints, which looked like they might cut through it at any time. I was certainly smaller.

My height still troubled me though, but there seemed little I could do about it. Amputation had an unrivalled permanence to it and I'd always rather liked walking.

As I waited for her to arrive, I began to wonder what came next. There were no more instructions. No plot constructed beyond tonight's gore. The manuscript seemed to cover the floor of every room now and it took me ages to gather all the pages of Chapter 14. I reminded myself of the detail before some last minute preparation. I opened the door. She was enormous.

'Hi,' I said. 'I'm Will.'

'I'm . . .'

'Rapunzel,' I said. 'You're Rapunzel.'

Seeing Anyone?

THE DAY STRETCHED out before him like some vast desert he didn't want to cross. The drive north to her house felt slow, somehow uphill, as if the car was subject to the earth's curvature. Choosing what to listen to was impossible; there was no music for this, so the last hundred miles passed in silence.

And then suddenly he was there, pulling into an unfamiliar driveway, in front of a cottage he'd pictured differently, with a garden they'd once dreamt of together. He turned the engine off, exhaled deeply and — now that it was too late — asked himself whether he should have come. Then she was standing there, smiling, as if he popped round every day. He picked up the envelope of photographs and the thirsty tiger lilies and stepped out.

'Hey, you,' Sarah said.

'Hey.'

They hugged clumsily. He waited for the musk of Chanel to hit him, but it didn't.

'You look well,' he said. 'Must be the country air.'

'You, too. Come on, come in.'

Following her inside, he was unable to resist a glance at a finger on her left hand, which he saw was bare.

Some of the furniture was familiar. A radio offered benign jazz that was barely audible. Smells competed for his attention: pungent ash from a recent fire, vinegary pickles and chutney wafting in from the kitchen, and the thick sweet scent of the oak beams.

'Here, let me put those in some water.'

'Wasn't sure what to bring.'

'They're beautiful. She's in the garden, under the tree. Coffee?'

The tree was a crab apple, which offered mottled shade. Curled up beneath it, on a worn tartan blanket, was the dog. He'd not seen her for three years. She heard him coming and tried to bark a warning, but was too weak. Then she recognised him, by his smell or face, he wasn't sure, and her tail beat slowly against the ground. The animal tried to get up but couldn't. He thought how old she looked. Much of her coat was grey and matted; her legs were like knotted sticks, her face gaunt. He stroked her head and she lifted it into his hand. As he moved his face nearer her, there was a smell he couldn't quite place—fetid and otherworldly, like death.

'The drugs make her stomach bloat like that,' Sarah said, handing him the coffee, a mug with a cow on it that he'd drunk from in another lifetime. She sat on the wooden bench next to them.

'Is Pete . . . ?'

'He's away,' she said. 'A golf weekend.'

He flashed a curious, almost judgemental look, and for a moment she indulged him before looking away, perhaps feeling disloyal. He considered whether Pete's absence changed the essence of his visit, whether he'd stay longer, whether they'd veer from small talk.

'Poor thing,' he said, turning back to the dog, who managed another wag. 'Wasn't sure she'd remember me.'

'They do.'

'What's the vet said?'

'A few days, probably. I have to decide when enough's enough for her, really. Not be selfish about it.'

'She's no age at all.'

'I didn't know whether to tell you. I thought about it for days.'

A warm breeze weaved between them carrying a small flower from the cherry blossom in the far corner. It caught in the strands of her hair like confetti, offering itself to him. He started to move his hand but it blew away.

For the first time he absorbed the fragrance and colour around him, wondering whether she was its sole architect, or if Pete had a say. The beds, he knew were hers. Peas and borlotti beans, peppers and tomatoes, stretched upwards, the last of the morning dew shimmering against the profusion of vermillion and green and ochre. A decked area was festooned with stone and marble pots. He recognised the two peach trees that were a tenth the size when he loaded them into the back of Pete's van in that other time. He'd asked to keep one, but she said they mated with each other and needed to be close, which he doubted. He remembered looking hard at her that day, trying to see if all her love for him had left, like a distant star that's seen but is no longer there.

'How've you been, Steve?' she said without looking up.

'Good. Yeah, good, really. You?'

'Things are good, really working out. We had to re-mortgage last year, when I got laid off, but we're picking ourselves up. You still teaching?'

'Gave up.'

'God, what . . . ?'

'Bought some Canadian canoes, me and Shaun take groups down the Tamar. This is our second season.'

'I can't believe you did it. I mean, well done. That's great.'

'Not had a headache since.'

A silence rose.

'Pete's business is starting to take off,' she said. 'He says this time next year . . .' She trailed off, leant forward in her chair and gently looped some hair on the dog's side round a finger. Their exchange, anodyne and synthetic, both surprised him yet was expected: the Doppler effect of love, where sound and language differ so much depending on whether it's arriving or departing.

'You're happy?' he said.

'Mmm, yeah, of course. Why wouldn't I be?'

'Sorry, I just meant . . .'

They both played with the rim of their cups for a while. He waited till her face softened, then: 'I brought these, don't know if you want to see them.'

She took the envelope and started to look through photographs of the first four years of the dog's life.

'I don't remember any of these.'

'We took so many.'

He let her study them without interruption, content to watch the emotions flicker across her face. By the end there was an ambivalence in her eyes, as if he'd dragged them back through time. She recovered and handed them back with a smile.

'I can copy any you want,' he said.

'I'd like that.'

'Do you remember how we chose her?' She did, of course, but played along anyway by not answering. 'That farm outside Totnes. The litter were all curled up at the back of a pigsty, sleeping. They all rushed to us, but then started to play with each other. She was the only one who stayed and nibbled our hands.'

'I preferred the markings on the other one, but you wouldn't hear of it,' she said.

Again he stole a longer look at her and noticed how much older her face looked. It could still take all the air from a man, but he realised how photographs and the memory kept the face at the age you last saw it. He remembered he used to think her beauty wasn't obvious, that you had to let it unfurl over time. But when truly seen, like a shape hidden within an optical illusion, you could see nothing else.

'Are you seeing anyone?' she said, looking down at the grass.

'Not really, no.' He was used to giving this answer to his parents, to friends. They teased and goaded him to expand on the 'not really', but today it just ushered in a silence, which he broke with: 'I'm happy, though.'

The homemade soup was like visiting his childhood home, its flavours awakening long-suppressed images and feelings. The only noise above the music was the occasional clinking of spoon on bowl and the breaking of bread. He wondered if she felt awkward in the silence, but neither of them filled it.

Back outside, they returned to the safety of unremarkable words—of respective families and old friends, innocuous anecdotes and world events. And then, as if by some trick of time, the shadows had lengthened and he was getting up to go.

He kissed the dog on the side of the head. 'Will you let me know when . . . ?'

'Of course,' Sarah said.

They hugged and he was sure the perfume of her skin and hair, of her, would crush him. He went to pull away, but she held on. Observed from a distance, it would have gone unnoticed, yet just by tensing her arms she seemed to change everything. He wondered how many moments made a life and whether this eclipsed all of them. He wanted to freeze the action. Say something, for fuck's sake. Find some words. But he didn't. Behind her, he took a last look at the cottage, their home, for a second allowing himself to traverse reality. He pictured himself in an upstairs window, watching as she tended the garden like a sculptor, the seasons wrapping them with their certainty as they aged together, suffused in love. Of all heaven's gifts, imagination was the cruellest.

She saw him out onto the road, the crunch of gravel deafening and damning. In the space between reversing and setting off, their eyes met.

Are you in love? Did you keep a picture of me? What are you reading? What is it that joins people? Where does it go? Could we . . . ? Could . . . ?

They didn't wave. He looked at her in the mirror watching to see if his brake lights came on.

The Games They Play

As he loaded the trolley with Cava and New World reds, Alex wondered how they would have played the game pre-motorisation and whether it'd been any easier to cheat. The keys, after all, were merely a tool—you could use anything, really. Surely, though, cheating was as old as the game itself.

It should have been enough, the prospect of a new couple, but it had been a libido-sapping week since learning his mother had a final laugh by leaving her estate to the PDSA. And so getting it up for most of the regulars would be difficult. Sure, one or two keys were still more eagerly felt for than others; an aesthetic pecking order went something like: Sue, Lucy, Meg, with Rachel and Frances joint last. (Alex felt mild guilt at placing his wife mid-table, caused mostly by the knowledge she would have him atop the men's.)

Occasionally a new set of keys would be introduced, the fresh meat at once petrified and excited as the room surveyed them with little subtlety: 'Everyone, I'd like you to meet . . .' Few stayed beyond a couple of months, once curiosity had been purged from their system, and so the group had remained the same for nearly a year now. Tonight, though, Lucy's veterinarian friend John and his wife Michelle were coming, and Alex knew wherever the latter came in rank, he had to fuck someone different this month. He had to have Michelle before the others got their grubby hands on her.

He'd mused for days on how to ensure he picked her. Keys, which on arrival were placed in a small box with a narrow opening, had to be homogenous in their lack of decoration, with no ornate rings or fobs that might be remembered from the last time and felt for. He'd practiced for ages trying to read like Braille the subtle indents of a Peugeot or Ford or Citroen logo, but with little success. Perhaps he could coat it with something once they arrived. But what? He wondered if it were possible to press the button on a fob from inside the box and unlock a car, see the lights blink through the window. Too elaborate. And he'd have to try all of them in theory—be like the Aurora Borealis in the courtyard.

It needed something simple and it was the sight of Meg spreading Philadelphia into a stick of celery that yielded hope.

'They didn't have the Rioja you like.'

Meg was finishing the vol-au-vents and canapés. She was all style and little substance, thought Alex. It still mattered to her the remarks each 'couple' made about her ability as a host once they left. She always fretted about the appearance of the whole sordid affair. The prospect of which odious man slobbered all over her mattered little as long as the domestics were beyond reproach.

'Do you still enjoy it?' she said out of the blue.

'What? Fucking other people?'

'All of it.'

'Yeah, I think so. Yeah. You?'

'I think so. It's just . . . '

'What?'

'I can't remember why we started.'

'I don't know, for the excitement. Because we were lonely. To recapture something. To feel alive again.'

'And do you? Feel alive?'

'Sometimes. Where are the damned flutes?'

'Perhaps we should stop.'

Alex had reckoned on this; he'd done well to go this long. A good run, really. The fact was that Meg was content with just him. Frivolous sex for her was almost a chore; she needed intimacy and tenderness, seduction and familiarity. Variety just didn't interest her. Given the choice, she'd rather be held all night, bathed in moonlight, than invite carnal oblivion. She went along with it to please him. Totally selfless. It was unreasonable to carry on indefinitely.

'Okay,' Alex said. 'But after tonight, yeah? Come on, they'll be here soon.'

Lucy and Steve were last to arrive, a trio of kisses on everyone's cheeks—lots of *darling how are you*s from Lucy, as if it were some society ball and half the room hadn't come in her in the last year or so. Alex, who came in her in August, craned his neck over David and Sue trying to glimpse the newbies Lucy had delivered them, but they had their backs to him. Meg was taking their coats, gushing away. He made his excuses and went over. For a moment he felt disappointment: Michelle, far from ugly, was still rather nondescript. Nothing of exception to her in any regard: medium height, neither fat nor thin—the plain woman you least remembered in a crowd. The only thing about her that turned Alex on was her obvious fear; her eyes betrayed a sanguine posture, alluding to a degree of coercion.

Alex remembered his first party, two years ago. It had been like one of those beer adverts: *Carlsberg don't do wife swapping, but if they did . . .* Meg had to be convinced over several months (the friends who'd introduced them were the last people you'd have down as swingers, and the disclosure took a while to ingest). Sentiments such as *We don't have to do anything if we don't want to* and *It might help things between us . . .*eventually won her around.

It had been like any other insipid dinner party in form; it was the undercurrent of the lascivious substance to come that gave him a hard-on all evening. In many ways it was more honest. When he'd chatted away inanely to women at parties before, he'd surreptitiously assess whether he wanted to sleep with them or not. Now this appraisal was transparent, practical.

The women had chosen that time, Alex's key plucked out by Sue, whose breasts had seemed to augment the more he drank. She was sober—the pickers, except the host, had to be to drive home—and to begin with their disparate tempos threatened to render the event too awkward to continue. In the end, they sat and talked till the early hours, Sue drinking, Alex sobering up, until an equilibrium was reached in which sex could occur.

The following morning, once home, he had tried to extract Meg's experience, but she remained reticent. He suspected she was entirely indifferent to the sex. After all, the men in the group certainly had the better deal, and Meg had spent the last fifteen years sleeping with the best of the bunch. But she never complained. Never seemed jealous. And it did spice things up with them. Sex the following day always had, for him at least, an edge to it, a ferocity that was part reclamation.

The next month he got Lucy (who was into McEwan, watercolours and submission); Frances for the two after that, which led him to suggest a rule (voted down) to prevent such repetition; then back to Sue, whose breasts lost most of their allure once their support was removed, and finally Rachel, who asked him to dress up in her husband's clothes, which, to Alex, seemed to defeat the point.

'This is John and Michelle,' Meg told Alex.

Michelle's husband seemed younger than her. Unlike his wife's, his eyes wore a hunger as he tried to scan the females in the room without getting caught—the boy in the chocolate factory. As they shook hands, Alex felt his own engulfed by the younger man's, whose effortless grip still suggested an ability to tear up phone books.

'We have to take your keys, I'm afraid,' said Meg.

'Get them some drinks, love, I'll do that.' Alex fetched the box, giving it a little shake. 'It could be you,' he said in his best baritone. John passed him the key. 'Our webcam's over there.'

As they looked anxiously across the room, Alex smeared the small ball of Blu Tack across the key's surface, just enough to fill the groove. 'Just kidding. Right, in she goes.'

He then took them around each couple, as if an auction were to follow. Mike was all over the new woman in seconds.

'We don't bite,' he said. 'Well, not to start with.'

'Ignore him,' said Rachel, looking down then up the new man. 'We won't let Michael pick you, my dear. Wouldn't be fair for your first time.'

'Darling. Do fuck off.'

'How long have you guys been coming, then?' said the new man.

Rachel's eyes gleamed with the double entendre potential, but Alex stepped in before she could open her mouth. 'We all started about the same time. Give or take. Come and meet David and Sue.'

By the time he'd shown them to everyone, Alex noticed how the reaction of the women towards John was unanimously effusive. And now, like little girls, they fawned about as the anecdotes spewed from the newest man. Meg came across with the drinks just as John had his hand inside a pregnant cow.

'How do you know she's ready to drop?' Sue asked.

'She'll be restless with labour pains,' said John. 'Her udder swells and its liquid goes milky. The vulva, too, is swollen.'

'Don't they come out on their own?' said Rachel.

'Mother Nature needs a hand sometimes. You have to wait till the first water bag is delivered and she starts straining her abdominal muscles. Lubricate your arms, pop them in and off you go . . .'

'Urgh,' said Mike.

'You need to help the mother dilate more, work your arm in and out of the birth canal for a while. I'm just there to help really, gentle pulls during contractions.'

'You must have very strong arms,' said Frances.

'Does it come out easily?' said Lucy.

'Not always. You have to find a leg first, count the joints—tells you which way round the calf is.'

'Does it matter?' said David.

'Much easier head first.' The women all hummed in accord. 'Had a heifer last week up at Monkleigh, hind legs first, poor thing had the umbilical cord round its neck. Managed to save it though, had to tie some rope around its feet and tail.'

'Wow,' said Sue.

'Incredible,' said Rachel.

'Amazing,' said Meg.

'You mustn't pull too hard,' continued John. 'Heard a

story of one farmer tying the rope to his Land Rover and putting his foot down. Big mess.'

Michelle wore the face of someone hearing this for the hundredth time. Her luck'll change later, thought Alex.

'It must be so rewarding, giving something new life,' said Meg.

'You implying he's there at the start of the process, Meg?' said Mike, laughing with the other men. 'How does that work, then, John? Need a step ladder, I suppose.'

'Can't take you anywhere,' said Rachel.

There was a pause. One of those lulls Alex always took delight in filling with slick repartee, caustic one-liners banked over the years. He had one for any purpose.

'I bet . . .' he began.

'So, Alex,' said John. 'What do you do?'

The whole room looked to Alex, for they weren't sure either.

'Do?' said Alex.

'You know, work?'

'Well, I . . .'

'He's between jobs,' said Meg, whether as rescue or sabotage, Alex couldn't determine.

It was all but midnight. Alex rang the bell and they gathered in the living room, all the women appearing like genies from a lamp. He brought the box in, placing it on the coffee table. He looked again at the new woman; even after a bottle and a half, he wasn't sure.

'Right, everyone, it's that time of night.' He shook the box. 'As you know, it's the men's turn, and being the host . . .'

'Get on with it.'

He reached inside, feigning indecision. His gaze swept around the room. Novelty still outscored the rest of this ordinary lot, he thought. After ten seconds or so he could feel no difference between the keys and panic started to set in. Not picking it wasn't disastrous in the sense of his own failure, but it meant the others would learn of his deceit.

'Come on,' said Rachel, 'some of us have other people's homes to go to.'

Then he felt something soft resist his nail and he pulled the key out, scraping the Blu Tack out with his thumb as he did so.

'Who's the lucky girl, then?' Alex said, passing the key to Sue to begin the inspection.

'Not mine,' she said.

'Nor mine,' said Lucy, a little too keenly for Alex's liking.

Frances looked genuinely upset on discovering it not to be hers.

And then Michelle took it, looking it over as if she wasn't sure and Alex wondered if he'd got rid of all the evidence.

'It's ours, I mean mine,' she said.

'Ya jammy bastard, Alex,' said Paul under his breath.

Alex offered Michelle his you-did-well smile.

'Right, who's next?' said Meg.

'Should be John,' said Rachel. 'The new boy.' The women nodded furiously in agreement. Alex tried to focus on having someone new in his bed tonight, but the nervous excitement spreading through half the room wouldn't let him. John stepped forward, his warrior hands having to squeeze through the hole in the box.

'W-who ya got, then?' said Mike into the silence.

John dangled the key, turning it on its ring, the light from the chandelier flickering from it as if it'd been whipped out of a river full of trout. The women all came closer.

'I think it's mine,' said Sue.

'No, it looks like ours, doesn't it Paul? Definitely ours,' said Frances.

They all looked at it, some twice, before retreating sullen-faced.

The first flecks of embarrassment were breaking out on John's neck when Meg stepped forward. 'It's mine,' she said.

There was audible relief from four of the men.

Alex looked at his wife's eyes, following their stare all the way to John's.

'Are you sure, darling?' he said. 'It doesn't look like . . .'

'Positive,' she said, smiling. 'It's mine.'

The Last Supper

THEY REMEMBERED THE meal now as if it were a long-deceased friend. Some details were embellished or forgotten, some flavours exaggerated. A course's description could still just about produce a glow in them. They tried to trick their woolly brains into conjuring the smells and colours. With no reference beyond a guess at the number of sunsets and rises, it was probably five weeks since they had consumed it, and nothing but water and each other had touched their lips since.

It had been exciting planning it, the knowledge it would be the last food their bodies and minds experienced proved both thrilling and overwhelming. They decided a day apart considering what to cook was necessary, before choosing the final dishes. He wanted monkfish, roasted in a caramel glaze. Her list opened with a rack of lamb, sauté artichokes with an almond tarragon dressing. He made a case for seared wild sea bass. She teased him, saying they could eat things that lived on land too.

He smiled and said: 'Duck breast in a red wine sauce.'

His piece of paper, once unfolded, said *Starter* and *Dessert*, meaning hers said *Main Course*. They shopped separately, prepared and cooked in silence. All other food in the house was collected and binned outside. Before serving, they began the seclusion. Both doors were double locked. The keys, along with those from the windows, were placed one at a time in the vice and bent out of recognition. He laid them in his palm and walked into the kitchen, showing her the contorted metallic sculpture. She smiled.

The letterbox was glued shut. The windows were covered with newspaper, as they both took a last look at the world.

'Let me do the phone,' she said.

She unplugged it and looked at him for approval.

He opened a drawer and handed her the scissors. They both knew a thing or two about temptation. The television got the same treatment. Only the CD player was spared as he placed disc three of *The Marriage of Figaro* in the open tray. She lit a solitary candle. Its flame boosted the late September dusk filtering weakly through last week's news.

'Shall we eat?' she said.

He wondered about the smoked salmon and dill blinis, for the first time feeling resentful at not picking the main dish. It was like being given a couple of short stories to consume whilst she gorged herself on a novel. As he spooned the crème fraîche onto the folds of salmon, the house was filled with horns and cellos and violas and Timpani drums. It reminded him of before they had been parents, when love was merely linear. When the current flowed backward and forth with no path to escape. No dilution. Selfish love, some might call it. That giddy time when love of self and another blur, when pleasure given is indistinguishable from that received. In some way they were now back to that time.

He remembered when she had taken him to Marrakech and they'd climbed the Atlas foothills on mules, an orange sun falling into the horizon. Just them and nature, as they stepped outside of everything they'd been a part of before they met, dismissing all else from a duet of solipsism. One by one, they dropped their friends; hobbies were forgotten, work neglected. An unspoken pact of hedonism secreted into each day.

A list of destinations was drawn up: the Caravaggios in Malta, Gaudi's Barcelona, St Mark's Square, the Inca trail, Angel Falls, the Norwegian fjords. They would feast their eyes on the world by day, and their bodies on each other at night. She took him to plays he'd never heard of, he read to her from his favourite novels. It was as if they were exchanging each other's very essence—the things that had made them who they were. A vacuum was created, inside which swirled art and music and literature and lust. They could have carried on forever. But then two became three.

She had excelled. A roasted loin of suckling pig was surrounded by garlic roasted potatoes in a grain mustard sauce. A small plate of green beans, walnuts and lemons sat next to a mixed endive and baby leaf salad. It seemed sacrilegious to disturb it. He topped up their glasses, for a second detecting some doubt in her eyes. The Rioja made the music hypnotic. Figaro's trial was just beginning.

Was it really more than a month since they'd eaten? He lifted her head gently and allowed some water to trickle from the glass into the groove of her closed lips. She parted them slightly and it disappeared. She felt colder than yesterday, as if her body's embers required stoking. Their skin was ashen, almost needing food's colour as well as its nutrients. He was unsure whether it was preferable to witness the symptoms in her first before he caught up a few days later. The fatigue and confusion, the muscle weakness, then convulsions and, yesterday, hallucinations.

'Shall I put some music on?' he said.

She shook her head and half smiled. Noise had become unbearable, but his desire to fuss over her was unremitting.

'Tell me about the meal again,' she whispered.

It had occurred to him to weep as he fetched the dessert, yet no tears were forthcoming. He'd used a high-roasted Arabica coffee bean with some dark rum to make the jellies. Amaretti cream lay to one side of the lustrous black domes, with mascarpone and pecan ice cream the other. She tasted hers, stood up, walked around the table and kissed him softly on the mouth.

The doorbell had sounded a lot recently, the sound seeming to skew and magnify as it cut through them like shrapnel. It was days before he thought to disconnect it. Voices accompanied the shadows that passed the windows. Occasionally, someone would shout their names, try a door handle. He supposed they'd break in eventually.

The room was infused with what he presumed to be moonlight, which made his heart ache. It seemed unlikely she'd see the morning. Maybe he wouldn't either. Crawling to the other bedroom for one last look, he paused outside the door. Inside, nothing had changed for a decade. Two Scalectrix cars remained frozen mid-race, an Action Man clung to the bed's headboard. Adventure books lay strewn along the dresser. On the far wall, below the clock that still said four twenty, was a crude drawing, now barely visible on yellowing paper. Three stick figures, their ridiculous heads like balloons on string, stood in front of a house. This house. Each wore a smile that overlapped their face. Beneath, in crayon, the words *I love Mummy I love Daddy.*

Three became two became none.

Busy. Come. Wait.

ALMOST THERE. TWO more bends in the lane and the east wall of the house appears through the poplars. Indistinct images of childhood scroll across my mind: falling from a bike, sliding in snow that had kept us from school, running into fields to escape custody battles. Jess will be there already, irked at my lateness, rehearsing caustic one-liners to fire off throughout the day. I park between her Golf and Dad's Volvo and see her at the end of the garden looking out across the estuary.

We hug fiercely, the kind reserved for once or twice a lifetime. For a moment I believe I can smell Dad on my sister, some residual semblance of the man. She pulls away and we turn to take in the house.

'When were you last here?' I ask.

'I come over most weeks. He needs someone to help out.' She realises the word implies a future, causing her eyes to water. She looks exhausted. I picture the hospital chair she'd spent several nights in.

'I tried to come up this year,' I say.

'It must be hard being so busy. Come on. I didn't want to go in until you got here.' She picks up the post and unlocks the door.

'Where's the cat?' I say.

'With neighbours.'

'We can't have him. I'd like to, but Jane's allergy . . . '

'Nobody asked you, Adam. They'll keep him until he can come to mine.'

The hall feels dank and unforgiving. A pitiless silence meets us.

'I feel like a burglar,' says Jess.

'Where do we start?'

'We don't have to rush.'

'I was hoping to drive back later.'

'Adam.'

'What?'

'Don't ask me to stay here alone tonight. I can't do it all.' I force a smile, which she takes as a concession. 'I'll put the heating on,' she continues. 'I want to wander around for a bit. Give me a little while.'

She heads towards the back of the house. In the living room the TV is on standby. I go to turn it off, decide to leave it on, then turn it off anyway. I pull back the curtains and another glimpse of childhood shoots through me: Mum collecting us for her turn, Jess hiding in the pampas grass, her white arms and legs tattooed with crimson nicks. Shouting, tears, then a compromise. I try to revive the memory, make the scene more vivid, but it fades to nothing.

The garden had been lost to arthritis. Once verdant and pristine flowerbeds are now parched, stifled beneath weeds. The pond is turbid and lifeless. Two shirts billow gently on the line as autumn slips through them. I sit on the arm of the sofa, close my eyes and strain to hear Christmas mornings unfurl—the first few we had here, when to a child all appeared wondrous and impregnable, cocooned as we were in naivety.

Floorboards creak above me. I follow my sister's movement as she enters each room. She's in hers now, the largest bedroom. We'd fought for it as children. I can't remember what promises had bought me off. I think I was supposed to have it after a couple of years, but never did. Her steps circle the room then stop by the window, giving us the same view.

I go through to the kitchen. The lack of dirty dishes cheers me until I see the stack of take-away boxes in the corner. I put some in the bin, hoping Jess hasn't seen them. I open the fridge. Half a pint of milk sits in the door; a tub of margarine and two cans of bitter have the shelves to themselves. By the phone is a note to ring Jess on Saturday. Pinned to a board are life's banalities: lists of long-forgotten DIY, receipts, a ten pounds book token, curled and yellowing. A calendar, unblemished except for my son's birthday, is months behind.

I call upstairs: 'Shall I start sorting stuff?'

'No, don't touch it, not yet.'

'We have to some time.'

'Not yet.'

I look around the dining room. Photographs I'd not noticed for years provoke enquiry. My children are winning the battle for space, then Jess, then me.

'Do you think Mum will want any of it?' I shout up.

'It's not hers to want,' Jess says, coming down the back stairs.

'She's stopped drinking.' Jess looks at me with an expression that either doubts this or renders it irrelevant.

'There's milk, shall I make us coffee?' I say. She stiffens as if this was sacrilegious, before her face softens to indecision. 'It's only milk.'

We sit at the dining room table, the clanking of hot water pipes bringing a little comfort as the house creaks into life.

'He never mentioned a Will,' says Jess. 'Hated all that. He would always say, Just help yourselves when I'm gone.'

'Is there anything in particular you want?'

'All of it. None of it.'

I look around the room. 'We could probably use the Welsh dresser, the bureau, maybe the . . .' She starts to cry, the enumeration too much. I reach a hand across to hers, but she pulls away.

'Sorry,' I say. 'I just . . .'

We sit in silence for a few moments until Jess breaks it.

'You should have come to the hospital.'

'I was going to. I thought we had longer.'

'You mean Dad had longer.'

'Yes.'

'You could have driven up last night, said goodbye.'

'Why? He was gone.'

'Christ, Adam. Stop being the pragmatist for one day.'

More silence.

'I presume you've told Mum,' she says.

'She was upset.' My sister chooses not to hear this. 'I said she was . . .'

'Why? Why was she upset?'

'Because she loved him once. Come on, Jess.'

'She didn't love anyone beyond herself. You don't have an affair and leave your children behind if you do. Who does that?'

'Most people, these days. And she didn't leave us behind. You could have come to stay when I did. There was always a bedroom for you.'

'I stayed a few times. Anyway, children shouldn't have to choose.'

'I didn't choose. It was sharing. She did her best. You're too harsh on her.'

'You're not harsh enough.'

I'd prepared for this on the drive up. Prepared for the last twenty-five years.

'Come on, let's start in the study,' I say.

She looks wounded by this, as if Dad's sanctum should be somehow preserved, untouched by marauding off-spring.

'There'll be bills to pay, paperwork,' I say.

The smell inside had changed little over the years. Stale pipe tobacco, a leather and mahogany swivel chair and walls of old books blend to give a bitter-sweet aroma. Dust hangs in the light that filters through the blind and Jess swishes an open hand through it before bringing it to her face. 'Isn't dust mostly skin?' she says.

As children we had to knock and wait to be told *Busy* or *Come* or *Wait*.

'You want to take that side?' I say.

There are totemic piles of *National Geographic*, photography magazines, *Reader's Digest*. A glass-fronted cabinet houses model Bentleys and Aston Martins; racing-green locomotives sit on a track that halts abruptly. There are more CDs these days, mostly jazz and blues, the occasional Verdi. Tobacco tins are home to copper rivets and washers, tiny nuts and bolts for securing whatever model kit he was assembling.

'Oh my god,' says Jess.

I go over. In a drawer, beneath several wallet folders, is a pile of pornographic magazines. I pull a few out.

'They're from the eighties,' I say, unsure what my point is.

'I'm just shocked, that's all.'

'He was on his own for years.'

'I know. It just feels . . .'

'What?'

'Some things you shouldn't know.'

'Look, we can do this another time if you want. Why don't you do another room?'

'Do you think there's more?'

'Porn?'

'Don't say that word. Yes.'

'Maybe. Does it matter?'

'I don't want that image in my head.'

'I'll get a bin bag.'

When I return Jess is thumbing through a frayed address book by the phone. She hands it to me. 'Can you do this bit?'

I only know about a third of the names, and most of those by reference. I begin with Barbara, who has no surname and just a mobile.

'Joe?' the woman cries.

'No, sorry, it's his son. Adam.'

She laughs a little then cries. She says her phone is set up to display a picture of whoever is ringing. She'd heard about Dad from a neighbour, so seeing him call shook her.

'Yesterday afternoon,' I say.

'Was it . . . ?'

'In his sleep,' I lie.

'We used to go to the park sometimes, feed the ducks,' she says.

'I'm sorry.'

I don't know what else to say, so ask if there is anything of Dad's she wants, which draws a scowl from Jess.

After an hour, I've spoken to most of them. We agree I'll do the rest in the morning. I ring home to say I'll not be back until tomorrow, then order us a Chinese.

'Get some wine,' Jess says.

We push prawns and noodles around our plates for half an hour, before giving up and opening the second bottle.

'Do you remember much when Mum was here?' I say.

'Bits. Fragments of drunken arguments, doors slamming.'

'Wasn't all like that. What about the zoo, you must remember the zoo. I was seven, so you were five. Remember it?'

'Not really.'

'I insisted on seeing the otters being fed, so we stood around in the cold for ages because we'd seen everything else and the keeper was late, so the otters thought we were going to feed them. They stood up on their back legs squealing at us. When he finally came, instead of giving them fish, he had a bucketful of dead mice and chicks, which he emptied into their little houses and we could see through the glass as they bit into them, guts spilling everywhere. You cried all the way home while Mum held you.'

'I can't remember going anywhere with them together.'

'We did lots. I think they were happy once.'

'So why give up so easily?'

'You can't stay together regardless.'

'So don't have children if you're going to call it a day soon after.'

'Six years isn't soon.'

'Why do you always have to defend her?'

I scrape the food into the bin and wonder if we can avoid sparring. I find her rolling a cigarette by the fireplace in the living room.

'Thought you gave up.'

'I have,' she says. 'Can we light the fire?'

'Doesn't look like it's been used for a while.'

'It'd be nice.'

I find some logs in the garage and break up an old chair for kindling. She was right—as the fire crackles and spits,

I realise the absence of sound had been intensifying everything. We now have something to focus on in the gaps.

'Mum will want to come to the funeral,' I say.

'Can't stop her.'

I feel some anger for the first time in weeks. Jess's intransigence is at best an over-reaction, at worst childish and tiresome. 'How do you know Dad didn't stray too?'

She thinks about this for a moment. 'Dogs stray, Adam.'

'Christ.'

'I don't want to talk about it anymore. I'm going to take those shirts off the line.'

'Do it in the morning.' But she's gone.

I consider the enormity of the house with one person inside. It was ridiculous that Dad kept it, rattling around like a janitor in a museum after hours. A house like this needs laughter resounding in it, children racing through its rooms. There'd been lodgers when Mum first left, to pay the mortgage, but Dad found the contrived politeness unbearable.

Jess is back, wearing one of the shirts, unbuttoned, over her jumper.

'Why do you think he never moved?' I say.

'He was always going to. Then it became too much for him. Easier just to stay. He didn't go in half the rooms. Stairs were hard.'

'We should have talked him into somewhere smaller.'

'It's our childhood home; those things are important. He wanted us to have as little disruption as possible.'

'But later, when we moved out.'

'I'm glad he stayed. It would have been horrible to lose this place just because Mum left. Things were bad enough.'

'Thought you didn't remember anything.'

'Maybe I remember some of it.'

'Like?'

'Let's leave it.'

'Fuck's sake, Jess.'

'Please, Adam.'

'Fuck, please. Look around, there are no marriages for life, people make mistakes, change; doesn't mean they don't love their children. You should forgive her. She's all we have left now.'

She gulps her wine and pours another. We are getting drunk too quickly. Another flashback: sneaking vodka upstairs for Jess and her friends when I could get served and she couldn't. I thought it'd ingratiate me with the pretty one.

I pick up her tobacco and papers.

'You, too?' she says.

'Sometimes. Jane doesn't know.'

'Family secrets, eh?

'Hardly.'

Jess watches as I try clumsily to roll the tobacco. When it won't stick, she points out I've used the wrong side and makes one for me.

'Do you remember,' she says, 'when I had tonsillitis? I was really young.'

'I don't . . .'

'You were away with Dad for the weekend, at Nan's I think. We were all supposed to go but I was really ill, so Mum stayed behind to look after me. I remember not being able to swallow anything. I woke up in the middle of the night, drenched in sweat, my nightie stuck to me. I went into Mum and Dad's room. Even though I felt terrible, I remember being happy because they were laughing and I hadn't heard them laugh for ages. More than laugh, they were playing, play fighting. I didn't want to spoil anything so I slipped under the sheets as quietly as I could and lay there really still. Their playing got faster and louder. I didn't mind; I was just happy not to be on my own. But then Mum started swearing, which made me scared. Do you know what she said?'

'You said me and Dad were away.'

'She said: "Fuck me. Fuck me really hard" over and over. I knew it was a bad word.'

'I don't understand.'

'I wanted to go, but knew if I moved they'd know I was there and they'd be cross with me, so I just put my fingers in my ears, but I could still hear them. Every now and then one of them would brush against me, but they were so drunk they didn't notice I was there. Although I had a fever, I started to shiver and I couldn't keep the sheets on me because Mum and Dad were moving so much. I put the corners in my mouth and bit hard, trying to keep warm. Then Dad started swearing, something like: "You fucking bitch, I love fucking you" and I realised it wasn't Dad and then I remembered he was away with you and now I was worried for Mum but I just lay there, quietly crying, wishing it would stop, wishing Dad was there to help Mum.'

Jess's eyes are manic now, her voice demented: ' "Fuck me, fuck me. I'm gonna come inside you, you dirty bitch, take it, take it all." '

I try to process her revelation.

'Then the fighting didn't seem like play fighting, so I said "Stop hurting my mum", but he didn't hear me so I screamed it as loudly as I could, which did the trick as he stopped hurting her. It was too dark to see him but I could smell his foul breath and feel his eyes on me. I thought he was going to start hurting me instead but it was just silent. Then Mum got out of bed, walked around, picked me up and carried me back to my room. I don't remember her saying anything, maybe she did. The next morning it felt like a bad dream and I just got on with being ill. I was six.'

'You had a fever . . . Maybe it was a dream.'

'I must have blanked it out, but when Mum left I knew I didn't want to live with her, just not why. It was years and years later—when a boy first kissed me properly—that I remembered. He tried to put his hand up my top and as he groped me his grunting took me straight back to that night.'

'She couldn't have known you were there.'

'So what? It was in Dad's bed. He'd been in it twenty-four hours before. And I was ill in the next room.'

'Why don't you talk to her about it?'

'To say what?'

'She might not even remember, the drink and all.' I play the events in my head again. I can vaguely remember the weekend at Nan's, being excited at going away with just Dad. But Jess's account, the climbing into bed unnoticed, seemed fanciful.

'You could talk to someone about it,' I say.

'You think I haven't.'

'A professional?'

'Plural.'

'Did it help?

'Oh, I managed to link it to all my failings as an adult, my inability to have a healthy relationship, the bastards I sleep with. Brought it all spewing to the surface. Help? God, no.'

'I'm sorry, Jess.'

'For what?'

'That it happened.'

'But you think I'm overreacting.'

'I think it was a long time ago. They both made mistakes.'

'Dad's mistake being going away for the weekend?'

The wine gone, I fetch the whisky we'd found in Dad's study. Unlike the milk, Jess finds solace in drinking from the same bottle.

'To Dad,' she says.

'To Dad.'

It burns going down and we both wince.

We discuss logistics some more, make a list for the coming days, as if grief had passed from one phase to the next. Jess talks about her latest faltering career, her fear of being alone forever.

We hug at the top of the stairs, a drunken embrace, Jess holding on this time.

'Have you even cried yet?' she says.

'Perhaps I'm scared to, case I can't stop.'

'You'd stop.'

As I lay in bed, the ache to see my wife and children overwhelms me, their significance intensifying more and more as today passes. As far as I can tell, we are happy. I know of no affairs or drug-taking or bullying at school. Do I take some credit for this? Certainly, I've used my parents as a model for how not to do things. Every new event, any matter that needed guidance or judgement, I'd check the blueprint my parents had given me and do the opposite. How I talked to my children, what I let them do. How often I bought Jane flowers, how I reacted when an affair offered itself. What would Mum or Dad do? I'd ask myself before not doing it. For years I'd even resisted having children, the fear that I'd inherited or learnt my parents' ability to fuck them up only eroded by a tender and patient wife.

I picture Jess across the landing. My little sister, who

like me still held on to some quaint monogamous ideal, yet could capture none of it for herself. I think of her as a child in the bed as Mum was fucked by Dad's brother or whoever was flavour of that month. Therapy had encouraged in Mum a pious devotion to spewing honesty onto anyone who'd listen, so over the years I'd endured her cathartic confessions, while watching any respect I'd had for my parents dissolve. If she was to be believed, neither of them had regarded marriage with particular reverence; Dad commencing the extra-marital activity shortly after Jess was born. He slept with half his colleagues and most of Mum's friends. In return she got his brother and anyone else who passed through. A happy little arrangement. Open and brazen. Only difference between them, it seems, was Dad hadn't been caught at it by his daughter, leaving him blameless in her eyes. A mother she hated because of what she knew; a father she loved because of what she didn't. By morning I will have decided if telling her might temper her judgement of Mum, or whether to let her keep the image of one parent intact.

I think back to the last time I slept here—two, three years ago. The kids had broken up. Jess was here with a boyfriend. Dad was on form—an old man but still in control of most of his life. Everyone had gone to bed except the two of us. We played chess, drank beer, dealt in small talk. The house was still, content at its rare glut of guests. There was a moment, several moves in, when I watched him closely, considering the board as if nothing else existed, impervious to the past, fearless of a lonely future, and I just chose to let everything go. All my judgements and criticisms. All my anger at a man whose best fell just short. I offered him no words, no ceremony, just an unseen smile as we played the night out.

They May Not Mean To But They Do

AUTUMN

I TELL THE DRIVER to stop a little shy of the gate and hand him twenty pounds. He hopes the ungodly hour means I'll forget the change, but I don't. As I get out, he mutters something under his breath, performs an ungainly three-point turn and drives off.

That was half an hour ago and I'm still staring at the house. Fat rain has found every weakness in my clothing, but I'm still not quite ready.

The phosphorous beam from the security light is broken by shards of rain. There are no lights on inside. I walk up the steps, get the spare key from under the plant pot and let myself in.

SPRING

You know how it is: you reach a certain age on your own and friends start inviting you to dinner, where mysteriously there is a fourth person of the opposite sex. She, as it happens, turns out to be single. 'Oh, we invited Clare / Maggie / Frances / Charlotte to make up the numbers. She likes Blake / Wagner / Venice / squash; you'll love her.'

I didn't, mostly. You don't get to thirty-six and find yourself still single by accident. I know they were trying to help, trying to do their bit. Matchmaking is so satisfying for some; it imbues them with purpose, with omnipotence. It's as if their creative bones can't stretch to any artistic endeavour, so they try to construct a couple. Then, when you're married and children arrive later, they can drone on about how they introduced you; how they always knew what a wonderful couple you would make.

For the most part I behaved. I took up my role with faux enthusiasm, grinning inanely at Clare / Maggie / Frances / Charlotte, listening to their vapid tales of how wonderful marketing / banking / teaching / counselling was. If I took their number, I deleted it before the taxi meter had moved. If I gave them mine, it would have an erroneous digit.

And then, at one such contrived gathering, when I was convinced the fatigue and depression of it all would render me into a welcome coma, I was introduced to Donna, and I knew, I knew before our host reached the soft vowel at her name end, that things would be different now.

WINTER

My name is (say name) and I've been here now for (say number of days). Smile sheepishly. Sit back down.

It's good to get in early in these hideous exchanges, otherwise your reservoir of *joie de vivre* quickly drains. Take Bill next to me. Last week we had to listen to his near-medical description of how he obtained alcohol on the outside in the absence of cash. The poor sod would tip lighter fluid down his neck with milk to keep it down just long enough for his stomach to absorb the alcohol before he vomited.

I prefer the cocktail of pills they give me, which provide emotional ballast, apparently.

Earlier, I was in the bathroom and all I could think about was that film with Jack Nicholson, where the huge Indian pulls the sink up from the floor and throws it through the window to escape.

I sense a pause: 'My name is Frank and I've been here now for ten days.' I sit down. There are twelve of us today. Graeme is our co-ordinator; he looks keen to see me open up.

'Do you want to tell us some more, Frank?' he says.

So I do.

SPRING

People who talk about finding their soul mate always rile me. What a misguided notion, that there's this one special person waiting for your paths to cross, that fate is driving you there. A pretentious friend of mine always talks in such cod philosophy: *When a relationship ends, it's because someone special is trying to find you.* If you were to challenge him, he'd offer you some green tea and call you a cynic, which I suppose I am. Until, that is, the dinner party the other night, where at the end of the evening I gave Donna my real number and wondered if I could bear the wait till she called.

As first dates go, it felt auspicious; none of the awkward pauses and fumbling and outdoing each other with benign topic starters. We quickly fell into sarcasm and teasing, as if we were old friends. Everything I said seemed to flow from my mouth as if I was the greatest door-to-door salesman of myself. We both laughed in all the right places and by dessert we were flirting with each other. Her laughs became giggles, my looks became lascivious.

That night I couldn't sleep. As we'd parted, I kissed her mouth, softly and for no time at all, and as I pulled away and looked into her eyes, it had been like looking into my own soul. It was like being seventeen again, but with the vocabulary to describe it.

AUTUMN

It's been several months since I've been here, but Dixon brushes against my leg, purring as if I've never been away. That it's four in the morning doesn't seem to matter to him. The mantel clock in the hall ticks away, its mechanism preparing for the half-hourly chime.

I think about growing-up here, the seasons flashing through my mind too quickly to fully observe. Smells and noises come to me: Christmases, endless summers with Mum pottering in the garden, Dad working on his Norton that never left the garage. I reflect on how little the house has changed, on how the spare room is still really my room.

Then I think of how different it should have all been and wonder what could make someone do that. I go upstairs.

SUMMER

Donna is inside me like a virus. Just a few months and the rest of my life now makes sense. Sometimes I just sit at my desk, watching her sleep, and want for nothing. It's as if we've been waiting all our lives to find each other, as if fate has driven us here. As far as I can tell, she feels the same. Being older played on her mind for a while, but I've never been drawn to younger women. What's a decade, I told her. I like someone who knows their own mind, who is a slave to their passion. With Donna it's her search for truth, and as we lay in each other's arms last night, I offered to help her find it.

WINTER

I finish my story and realize everyone is staring at me. My words have jolted them from chemically-induced trances. Even Graeme has stopped making notes and looks like he's seen a long-dead relative.

'What?' I shout at them, but it's like I've told them I'm the messiah and they believe me.

SUMMER

For many it doesn't matter where you come from, it's who was there that counts. And Donna thought this way once. But something changed within her and now she searches. In libraries, on the internet, records offices — whenever time allows, she looks for the parents who gave up on her when she was three days old.

I wonder if I'd do the same, if I'd want to know. What would be the point? It's only DNA. And what when you've found them? Why would they want to know anymore now? What words could possibly be sufficient?

But when you love someone, when you've explored every beautiful and intimate part of them, it doesn't matter what you think. I would do anything for her.

SPRING

Donna just said she is falling in love with me. Yeats comes to mind: *Tread softly because you tread on my dreams.*

SUMMER

Finally the envelope is here. She starts to open it but is too nervous. I do it for her. I want to be as much a part of this as possible.

'I love you,' I say, and look at the letter. Half way down, I see my name. Not all of it. Just the surname. Twice.

AUTUMN

I look at my parents, cocooned by each other and the duvet. Rain drips from my hair onto the carpet. Finally sensing something, my mother wakes and sees me.

'Darling,' she says. 'What is it?'

WINTER

I leave the others to their stupor and madness and shuffle to the bathroom, my feet barely leaving the floor. Once there, I place my arms under the sink and try to find the strength to pull it free.

Old Enough

THE FRONT DOOR bangs shut and the house is mine. I imagine Clare's school bag dragging behind her as her brother tells her again that they'll miss the bus. In four years, since they both became old enough to deliver themselves to places, they've only missed it once. Clare had slipped on the ice, gashing her knee, and they'd watched the snow turn red, listening to the bus weave its way to Tavistock without them. I'd opened the door to her crying, Paul annoyed at the prospect of me or their father dropping them at the gates for friends to see.

They'll both be cold today—Clare because she's Clare, Paul because it's not fashionable to wear a coat. Winter on the moor is for the hardy, and I wonder if my children will one day forgive me for the life I've given them.

I stack the breakfast plates and Robert's cup in the sink before making a strong coffee. Standing at the window, watching the wind-combed trees in the woods to the north, the nausea returns for the first time in years. I pick up my coffee and go into the studio, where a pale winter sun falls on yesterday's pots.

The exhibition is six days away, highlighted on my calendar with a sweep of vermillion. I finish loading the kiln with some plates that will wait patiently for the temperature to peak at eleven hundred degrees. This first firing done, they can then be given some colour and life.

A Radio 4 play feels stilted, so I opt for silence, before

preparing some body stains. I need to be consumed by work today, for it to envelop me like a hot air balloon that has collapsed on its basket. But you can't stop the mind; it's as if by trying to, you highlight the danger. So when I tell myself the man in the market crowd yesterday couldn't have been him, that I'm just seeing ghosts, my mind suggests that it was.

'Get off, Mum,' Paul had said earlier, as my fierce hug went unreciprocated.

I asked him what time he'd be home, whether he was going to a friend's after school, but he chose not to hear me.

Robert knows something is wrong, but will wait for me to reveal what. I am grateful the exhibition allows me to go to bed hours after him. In his sleep he touches me, or makes himself hard with my hand before I withdraw it. A forlorn look in the morning, or no look at all, tells me his mind retains these exchanges on some level.

I look at the photograph of him on the notice board, his eyes following me around the studio. There's nowhere in the room he can't see me.

I sit on the stool, staring at a bowl sitting expectantly on the wheel, and suddenly I loathe how it needs me, how it cannot flourish or fulfil itself without me. Turning to find a brush, I knock over the coffee. Splashes dapple themselves onto the bowl's porous surface, creating unbridled patterns. I contemplate its artistic merit, the accidental versus the deliberate, before hurling it across the room. It hits the far wall and falls to the floor in shards. I breathe deeply. The anger tries to find a foothold, but instead falls away.

My eyes well up. I walk to the mirror in the hall, almost in fascination. I can't remember the last time I cried. The tears snake down one cheek, then the other.

There's a pause, a consideration, before they drop one at a time onto my shirt.

I go back into the studio and sit facing the photograph of my husband. He would hate me to call him beautiful, but he is. Not just in the way a father holding his children can be, but his features have a symmetry, a grace that is almost feminine.

I find myself talking to him. I want to see if his face changes at all, if he can bear this new truth. I tell him about a young woman in her first real job sixteen years ago, about how she was going to change the world with her love of books.

I was twenty-three, battling a fatigue with a large glass of Shiraz. As trainee teachers we had a taste of the hours needed after lessons. But you finish at half three, you lot. No, I'd thought, we come home at half three.

The buzzer of my first-floor flat resounded above Joni Mitchell. I lifted the receiver, pushed the small button and called him up.

Can I have a glass, Miss? I remember his emphasis on Miss even now. I told him to call me Anna—it felt egalitarian. He didn't, though.

It had been my idea, not two months into the job: a few hours a week for the few disruptive ones showing any promise. I wrote to Jamie's parents and each Tuesday at seven I tried to tease out some literary creature from within him.

Just a half, I replied. I presumed he'd drunk beer or cider with friends, and reasoned that Harper Lee should be savoured with something other than coke or instant coffee. It was meant as a gesture—a device to undermine the formality, to encourage a productive session. The judge called it naïve.

I turned the music down and we sat at the table in my kitchen-diner. Jamie was one of two boys I tutored privately. Both were troublesome, both occasionally produced meritorious work. And although Jamie's beacon was the paler, it was him I could see shining one day.

The lessons were a welcome distraction. Affairs were something I thought happened to other people. But when you're lonely and in a new city, a little charm is easy to succumb to. Nick came here twice a week after work, but I'd put him off recently. His parting words last week left me resolved to end it: *You're wasting your time with those two, Anna. You can't change someone's nature . . .* he'd said, pulling tight the plum tie that alluded to domestic bliss elsewhere.

Jamie swigged his wine with little finesse and slumped back in his chair, winking at me. I told him to stop messing around. I asked him if he'd read the end of the trial, as we'd agreed. He stared at me as if my words were rhetorical and I wondered if I *could* change his nature, whether I should have even been trying. Perhaps it was middle-class guilt—seeing his worn uniform, his scuffed shoes, knowing about his problems at home—that gave me the arrogance to think literature was a panacea; that my gift of words to him could turn his life around and he'd one day drop my name into conversations about how wild he used to be.

Can we watch a film, Miss?

Seeing he'd come without a bag, I leant back in my chair, scanned the bookcase, and pulled out my edition. I tossed it across the table and it fell in his lap. *Go on, then,* I said. Chapter 18.

He flicked through the pages with indifference, stopping to look up as if his task were complete, but I left the space empty for him to fill with a laboured sigh and eventually some words.

Thomas Robinson reached around ran his fingers under his left arm and lifted it he guided his arm to the Bible and . . .

I snatched the book from him and said: *Slowly. Savour the words—it's not a shopping list: Thomas Robinson reached around comma—ran his fingers under his left arm and lifted it full stop—he guided his arm to the Bible . . .* I passed the book back.

It's fucking boring, he said.

That's because you're saying the words without thinking about them.

He loosened his already slack tie further, flicked his fringe out of his eyes and scanned the room. He took his cigarettes out. I raised my eyebrows and he put the packet away with a grunt. For the first time, a tension between us rose from the silence. I reminded myself this wasn't supposed to be easy.

How old are you? he asked.

Old enough, I said.

He chewed on the answer for a while, then: *They said you done it with Mr Youngs. That he's gonna leave his missus for you.*

Disarmed, I tried to formulate a response, but my vocal cords were paralysed as my mind flashed through all the implications, like a thumb rippling a deck of cards. Images of whispering colleagues in the staff-room morphed into a playground of taunting pupils.

Seems you're not old enough to ignore playground gossip, I said.

Don't matter, Miss. I've done it loads, too. I'm old for my age. Do you take him in your mouth?

And then what? It's always the next bit that's opaque. The grey minute, as the defence called it—a time of confused signals and forgotten roles. I think I told him to leave. I remember realising I was a little drunk. He threw the book on the floor. I followed him to the door, questioning teaching's virtuous claims. I pictured my mother, her penchant for rescuing fallen men and stray animals seemingly genetic. As we got there, Jamie leant forward, kissing me clumsily on the mouth. I jumped back, like a calf recoiling from an electric fence.

Jamie, I . . .

He pushed me into the wall and kissed me again, harder. I tried to get free but his hands held my head like a vice. There was a sense of it being a dream, like something you read about. I closed my lips as tightly as I could. He gave up trying to kiss me and put a hand on my breast, his eyes a study of fascination watching his fingers squeeze me. Once I slapped his face, there hung a pause, as if neither of us knew what to do or say. He backed away, just a step or two, but kept eye contact. The mischievous look in his eyes had gone, replaced by something I'd not seen before and haven't since.

Come on, I said, and reached for the door, but I found myself on the ground, my senses trying to re-plot the room's co-ordinates. I realised he'd punched me. A shrill note ricocheted off the walls of my skull and I tried to focus on something static. I remember the taste of warm copper in my mouth as I sputtered out a mulch of blood. He forced me onto my front and pulled my head back by its hair, before slamming it into the floor. A black screen appeared, interspersed with brilliant white specks, flashes that exploded like stars, before fading and appearing elsewhere. I came round to a smell: not unpleasant at all. Fragrant. As his hair danced on my cheek, I realised it was shampoo. Another sensation: cold, like ice, a belt buckle against my thigh. Then black again. It felt as if I was swimming to the surface, sound dulled, then bursting through, back into the room. There was a tear of fabric. My body contorted as if choking, defending itself. I tried to crawl forward, but his weight was too great. Bizarrely, I recalled a woman in a documentary talking of least resistance, whilst another spoke of fighting to the death. I knew what was happening, yet it was like there'd been some mistake, that it would just stop any minute. I even called his name out with a laugh, as if he could be reasoned with, as if this silly game had gone too far now. Then he was inside me. I screamed: a visceral, animal cry. *Jamie, no. No, Jamie. Please. Stop.* His grunts were so angry as he slammed into the back of me. I tried to crawl away again, but he pulled my hair with one hand and looped his other arm around my throat. His breath smelled of cigarettes and wine. Everything went black for a second. He pulled out too far and it took him several attempts to penetrate me again. There was less pain now, but I could hardly breathe. He started shouting: *Bitch fucking bitch.* An image of my father appeared, frantically sawing wood. I tried to focus on it. Tried to leave my body behind. I started to choke. *Fucking bitch.* The sawing sped up, then stuttered, then stopped. His full weight fell on my back. He released my neck and I blacked out.

I came to. I took the absence of pain to mean I had died. In the distance a waterfall cascaded into a violet lagoon. No, not a waterfall. Something else. A man pissing. A boy pissing. The gap where a flush should have sounded was filled with the distinctive lighting of a Zippo: *click, flick, click.*

Silence. A door slammed shut. I remember making out the word *Mockingbird* on the book's spine.

I'm brought back to my studio by the faint smell of

sulphur as the clay begins to oxidize, the final molecules of water abandoning the plates. Beyond the kiln, outside in the silver birch, a blackbird studies me. Its orange-yellow beak starts to release a song, but it decides against it and flies away. I look hard through my tears into my husband's eyes. My family, their oblivious joy captured in the blink of a shutter.

The exhibition is well attended. The effusive gallery manager is directing people to the canapés and champagne in the knowledge they'll buy more after a glass or two. The soft lighting, the jazz drifting through the room—it's all part of the sales package. I both hate and need these events.

Everyone wants a piece of me, expecting me to talk of creative procedures, to reveal sources of inspiration. They want to be able to say to friends who see my piece in their lounge that they've conversed with its creator.

Robert looks at me from across the room and smiles. I know he can see the fear in my eyes. I think of all the times I've nearly told him and whether the absence of truth is always a lie.

Following him around and looking increasingly bored are Paul and Clare. It's an excuse to stay out late, but both would rather be elsewhere. Despite the five years between them, despite them sharing only one parent, they are incredibly close.

Knowing I love them both equally seems to relax me for the first time in days. And then across the room I see him. He's just standing there, looking at one of my plates, examining it hard as if the pattern held some code.

I start to feel hot and sick. The room begins to swirl, the floor seems to ripple, as if I were on the deck of a ship. Unlike the market, I know it's him this time. Some people pass through the space between us, and when I can see him again he's looking up around the room. His glasses and closely cut hair almost hide him, but his eyes are the same at thirty as fifteen.

'Wonderful pieces, Anna,' a woman I can't place says, but I ignore her.

Has he really looked for me, for us? My name is different. I look different. And then he's walking towards me, brochure in one hand, glass in the other. I'm screaming inside; it's so loud, I can't believe no one is looking at me. He's ten feet away now. Eight. Six. My legs can hardly hold me up. My hands are shaking. I bite my bottom lip hard until I taste blood. I try to make my eyes look elsewhere but they won't. I wait for him to do whatever he's going to do. But he just walks past. He doesn't even look at me. I don't turn around, but I can sense him getting farther away. I force myself to turn and I see him heading towards the gallery's front door. And then he's gone.

Robert is by me now, asking if I'm okay. I tell him I'm not sure. He says he'll get me some water.

It was him, I tell myself. *It was Jamie.* And as if to check, I look across the room at my son's face.

There Are New Birthdays Now

MARY CALLED UP to Ben that his coffee was all but cold, that he should leave before the roads snarled up. He opened the boys' door, allowing the room's scent to grace him for a moment before going downstairs.

'Did you sleep at all?' his wife said, last night's anxiety in her voice gone or hidden.

'A little. Did they get off alright?'

'Of course.'

'And they know you're picking them up if I'm late back?'

'Yes.'

'And they know to wait inside?'

'Ben . . .'

'Sorry.'

'You should have some food before the drive. I made you a flask.'

He wanted the car to be older and smaller. It reeked of family. Of a secure, contented nuclear family, which he supposed they were. Stopping at a service station, he detached the child seats, placing them out of sight in the boot. She might not even see the car, but doing it brought comfort.

After they'd separated, he still saw his first wife

regularly. Meetings with police, a counsellor they saw together before finding their own. There'd also been contact whenever something went wrong in her life. Small things: a burst pipe, which he went round to fix; some problem neighbours. Other times he'd just be summoned and they'd sit there in swollen silence until he felt able to leave. But when he told her he'd met someone, there was nothing. Certain dates would bring silent phone calls, which Ben assumed were her, while Mary laughed them off as wrong numbers. It was when their cat went missing that they decided to move. No reference to anything, no accusations, just that a clean start away from it all would be good. Barely anyone was told: family, a few friends. They scuttled away, unnoticed.

When the calls began again two weeks ago, he supposed she'd found them. Wasn't difficult these days, personal details strewn across the Internet if you knew where to look. And then a letter, oddly warm, asking to meet. Her address was different, he saw. (It surprised him she stayed in the house as long as she did.) He considered ignoring it, or sending a polite reply without Mary knowing. But they'd said at the start: no secrets.

The letter hadn't asked for a response, offering instead a place and time to meet, a coffee shop near their old address. He couldn't place it, guessing one of the old bookshops had perhaps perished. *You can't miss it*, she assured him. The postscript said she knew he'd come.

'What do you think she wants?' Mary had asked.

'I don't know.'

'Surely anything could have been said in the letter.'

'It's probably nothing.'

'Why now, after all this time? Why that day?'

Ben paused. 'It would have been her birthday.' He saw that the tense confused Mary for a moment, before her face softened and she came and sat next to him, taking his hand.

'I didn't think. Which one?'

He looked upwards, calculating. 'Sixteenth.'

The birth of the boys had almost expunged the date from his mind, to the extent that he'd often notice it only once it had passed. For the first couple of years he and Jan had acknowledged the day, making a cake they never ate, perusing photo albums until it became too painful. But there were new birthdays now. For him, at least.

'Will you go?' Mary had asked.

'Yes.'

The roundabout confused him; it hadn't been there before. Traffic was now sent alongside the river through what had been wasteland. Nothing remained of the gorse that had been searched so meticulously, the line of men and women on their hands and knees striking him as absurd now. They found nothing, save a child's shoe that wasn't hers.

The letter had said that she still didn't drive, that if he could come to her it would be better. Public transport could have taken her anywhere of course, somewhere benign, but she wanted him to return and he had no desire to negotiate.

Driving along the High Street, he wondered whether people would be familiar. It had been eight years, but he knew the faces in small towns changed little. He welcomed the anonymity of the car and hoped the coffee shop would be quiet; it had been so long since he'd been recognised by strangers and he cared little for it. Occasionally a journalist picked up the story on an anniversary or when something similar happened elsewhere—they were still worthy of a feature, if not news. It's why he took

Mary's name when they married, to stop the double takes when you filled in a form or introduced yourself. And it wasn't fair on the boys to be labelled. To have a surname that was ghostly.

At first there'd been nothing but sympathy, attempts to share the grief. *How could this have happened?* they said. *The sheer horror of it all.* But then, slowly, when nothing was found and time bellowed with the absence of news, the glare turned inwards, towards them. Disapproval appeared on faces. Questions reverberated from pockets of gossiping neighbours. *How could they be so careless? Had they been drinking?* Blame began to shift from some unseen stranger towards them. People needed their object of hate to have substance. *Perhaps they even had something to do with it*, became the subtext.

He parked in a quiet terraced street, found a meter and put money in for two hours, wondering if this was too much or too little.

It was right where she said, a trendy frontage boasting exotic teas and organic juices. He was grateful the door didn't have a bell or rattle on opening. A few people were scattered about, their sum proving neither busy nor quiet. He weaved through them, avoiding eye contact, and ordered a latte. A cursory sweep showed no sign of her, no singly occupied tables, so he sat in the corner seat.

It occurred to him to turn his phone off and as he did someone approached from the side.

'Hello, Ben.' His ex-wife stood there, bottle of beer in hand.

'Jan. I didn't see you when I came in.'

'Nipped out for a smoke. Can you believe we have to huddle round outside these days like some underclass?'

'I gave up.'

'Oh.' She sat down opposite him, moving the menu to one side. 'Let's have a good look at you, then,' she said, sitting back.

He'd been anxious that their conversation wouldn't be strictly private, but there appeared enough space and background music between them and the nearest occupied table.

Ben's first thought was how she'd aged, how she looked ten, maybe more, years older than Mary, despite being younger by a year.

'How are you, Jan?'

'I'm alright. You look well.'

'Thank you.'

'How's what's her name?'

'Mary.'

'Yeah, Mary. Such a pretty name, I always thought. You did well.'

'She's good. How about you, did you ever . . . ?'

'Take a look, Ben. Years haven't exactly been kind.' If this was an invitation to be contrary, he didn't take it.

Her hair—flecked with grey, its lustre gone—was drawn back tightly so that the blanched skin gave her face a cold leanness. Her features appeared taut, as if gripping the anguish that had penetrated them; even a forced smile drew attention to the perennial grief around it. Ben had kept no photographs when they moved, not of Jan anyway, and he found it hard to conjure up an image of the woman he'd once loved.

'Life been kind to you, Ben?'

'I'm okay.'

'Nothing much changed here. Same old, same old.'

He thought of something to say, telling himself it was bound to be awkward.

'Dad died last year,' Jan continued.

'I'm sorry.'

'The stress didn't help, they said. That and the fags.'

'Your mother still . . . ?'

'She'll go on forever. Longer than us, I reckon. Yours?'

'Good, yeah, they're good.'

A silence gathered, Jan's unblinking eyes fixed on his.

'Are you going to have another drink?' he asked.

He'd barely sat back down when Jan said: 'You had any more, then?' Her words should have been absurd, absent of context, yet he understood.

'Children?'

'No, heart attacks. Course children.'

He looked down, trying to formulate a response.

'It's okay. I don't mind,' she said.

Looking up, he nodded. 'Two,' he said, before quickly adding: 'Boys.'

'How old?'

'Four and five.'

She stared at him expectantly, as if he hadn't finished. 'Do they have names?'

'Matthew. Matthew and Peter.'

'Aw, that's lovely. Got any pictures?'

'No,' he lied.

'Bet they look just like their father.' He swilled the last of his coffee around, watching keenly the frothy patterns it made. 'Do you still think about her, Ben?'

'Of course.'

'She's still alive, you know.'

'Jan . . .'

'Ask me how I know.'

'How?' he said, wearily.

'A mother does. I'd know if something happened to her. No, she'll be meeting a boy tonight somewhere, in some hot place, a birthday dinner. He'll be shy, not pushy. He'll offer to pay, but she won't let him, so they go halves. It's her first real date. Just getting into boys, she is. Won't hand it to them on a plate. Has respect for herself.'

Ben thought it pointless to say that, were she alive, she'd have a new birthday now. A date plucked from the air, maybe a year or more wrong. That was the best scenario, that whoever took her did so out of a yearning emptiness, to replace a loss of their own. That somehow she'd been taken out of the country and had given love to another couple. The police had always maintained this was unlikely.

'Why did you want to meet, Jan?'

'I thought we could go for a walk.'

As a child, Ben had always lost things: dinner money, inhalers, a watch his parents had bought him. He remembered not quite believing his eyes at first, thinking that Jan had brought her in, even though he knew she hadn't. Or that the hydrangeas were obscuring his view, even though it was late autumn and both were near bare. There was a bird, a song thrush maybe, where she should have been, alertly hopping around her doll as it foraged. The police kept asking how long the gap was between seeing her and not, but it was impossible to say. Five, six minutes. No more than ten. One of them, the older of the two, smiled warmly while his colleague remained impassive as he took notes. These roles changed little over the weeks and months, especially when difficult questions, as they called them, had to be put. *There was just a bird*, Ben kept saying. Without looking up, the younger one had asked how old she was. *Three*, said Jan, as she stared hard at Ben. *Almost three and a half.*

He knew immediately where they were going. He could have refused, chosen not to indulge her, but part of him, the piece lured by atonement, drove him on.

'For years,' Jan said, 'before I moved, I'd look out a window and see someone taking pictures. Not just press; ordinary people, like tourists, wanting to see the garden, the house, as if it was a bloody pilgrimage or something.'

'I don't remember that.'

'You went straight back to work, hid away in your little office.'

'It seemed better to get on with things. I felt powerless at home.'

They crossed West Park Road, heading past the two pubs he hadn't gone in again. The streets were quiet; occasional passers-by made him lower his head. He noticed Jan held hers high, sucking hard on a cigarette.

'A young couple bought it. He ran his own business, I think he said. Can't remember about her. They knew, of course, you could tell. I made tea as they were shown around and I could feel their tension as they walked about in silence upstairs. It's nice to think someone else is using it.'

'The house?'

'Her room. It was empty for so long. Rooms need people in them.'

'How do you know it's not empty now?'

'I watch them. They had a daughter; she'll be five, no six. Lovely fair hair . . .'

'Christ, Jan.'

'I know, it's strange, isn't it? Given what happened. You remember the bus stop by the alleyway? You can stand there and see right up the garden and nobody thinks anything of it. It's where they would have watched from.'

There had been no witnesses. Nobody saw a thing, but

it was assumed the person or people went up the alley, perhaps a car with its engine running waiting on Eliot Road.

As they neared the house, Ben expected a terror to grip him, but in some sense he felt like one of the tourists, taking a macabre peak at the scene of the crime, as if it had happened to someone else.

'You over the other side of town now, I see,' he said.

'I would have stayed, but the mortgage . . . '

'Why would you want to stay?'

'You know why. For when she comes back. How would she know where to go?'

They rounded the corner and he could see the driveway. Jan led them to the bus stop where, fortunately, nobody was waiting.

'What if a bus comes?'

'We wave it on.'

As they got there, Ben looked along the alley. Litter-strewn, occasional graffiti, it seemed the epitome of commonplace, yet it was a portal to another world. He scoured the banal fascias of the houses in each direction. All those windows and front gardens. All those families. How had nobody seen anything?

He noticed there was a car in the drive.

'Oh, they'll be in,' Jan said. 'He works from home now; she finishes at one.'

'We should go.'

'One of them walks to school at ten past three.'

'Jan, please.'

'If it's raining, she drives. Lazy really, given the distance.'

'They'll see us looking.'

'I would have walked, if, you know . . .'

'I'm going, Jan.'

'I think they've redecorated her room. Looks violet now. New lampshade, too.'

He forced himself to look up at the front of their old house. It looked both the same and different. The sash windows now plastic. The silver birch gone. But still the same.

'You'd think they'd have put a fence up or something,' said Jan. 'You know, case lightening strikes twice.'

For a moment he was aware of the sound of Jan's words, but not their meaning. His shirt, sodden with sweat, clung to his back. He thought he might be sick.

'We always left her in the garden for a few minutes,' he heard himself saying. 'People did.'

'I like what they've done with the beds. We always neglected the front.'

'No way it was more than ten minutes.'

'They fixed those loose tiles, too. Look.'

'You could have checked from an upstairs window. You knew she was outside as well.'

'Come on, Ben. You knew I was busy. You were watching her.'

He looked at Jan. For all her torment she spoke with a calmness that suggested insanity. Not the frenzied madness of that time, when she'd scream and scratch and spit at him. Blame him. There was a cold detachment from reality now, a dementia. She was right though; he'd known she was busy.

'Are you crying, Ben? Don't be sad, it's her birthday.'

Driving back, he tried to keep out thoughts of his daughter. Unlike Jan, Ben's image of her never aged, never grew up; she remained frozen in time, a face on a hundred posters. For most, he thought, death is cruel in its haste, rarely warning of its arrival, certainty its only compensation. But death revealed itself to them in episodes, and then never fully. It would linger above them, festering for days and weeks, its presence threatening to engulf them, before vanishing, swept away by ephemeral hope. The sightings all came to nothing though, and in the end he'd chosen to welcome its return.

And now he preferred to think of that time as a novel he'd read. You had to put things in boxes.

Mary smiled through the living room window as he pulled into the drive, the diffuse light behind her giving his wife an ethereal, haloed quality. She had been his saviour at a time when he sought life's ordinariness, when mundanity was sacred. He thought of how he'd entered her life with such a public narrative; like everyone else, she'd followed the story on television, in the papers, from the appeals and press conferences. It was baggage and yet he brought nothing tangible—no maintenance orders, no access disputes, no weekend visits. There was nothing that bound him to his first marriage other than the power of an event.

Years passed before Mary had broached the subject of a family, her patience with him as profound as her belief in his innocence. 'There's no rush,' she'd said. At times she would quietly point out when his obsessive desire to protect the boys, to cocoon them, became overzealous, damaging.

He pictured Jan standing at the bus stop year after year, watching happiness play out in others, a new life seemingly beyond her. Her reaction on hearing about the boys was so understated that he considered if somehow she had known. Perhaps their old house wasn't the only place she watched. He would talk to Mary about moving again. Further away this time.

He'd hugged Jan as they parted and she'd held on

longer than him, for a moment belying her blithe tone. He had never asked her forgiveness and now never would.

'What do you want?' he'd said, wondering if today was an end of it.

'A family, Ben. Same as you, that's all.'

He opened the front door and called up to the boys that he was home

Staring at the Sun

EIGHT-TEN. SHE'S late and a million doubts flash through me. Still only fashionably so, but much longer and I'll suspect the worst.

'How will I recognize you?' she'd asked.

'I don't have a beard and I'll look nervous.'

'Me too,' she'd laughed.

I search for a balance between drinking my pint and looking as if I haven't been sitting here for ages. The clock above the optics taunts me. Its Roman numerals are mirrored so that backwards is forwards. It's funny: the long hours of today lumbered by like the desert sun tracking slowly across the sky; now the minutes hurtle past as if they've somewhere else to be. Got to slow them down. Like the poem. *Stop all the clocks*. Moving ones tick slower apparently, but I can hardly take it from the wall.

Not everyone surrenders to time with servile obedience; one or two have cheated its mastery. There's a cosmonaut who's travelled into the future. Not much—about a fiftieth of a second—but he's younger now than if he'd stayed on Earth.

Given the choice I'd still go back, not forward. The past is where everything I know exists: love and joy, pain and loss. It's all I have to tell me who I am. Why would I want to let it go?

We'd moved in with Jane's parents to make it easier at the end. She used to sleep for days at a time, so I'd just read by her bedside. I found a book on her father's shelves about a caver who spent sixty-three days underground. With no clues as to day or night, he chose when to eat, when to sleep, when to be active, and would radio up to tell his team when his days began and ended. You'd think he'd lose all track, but even his body remained loyal to a twenty-four-hour cycle, give or take a few minutes. By the end he was only a couple of days out.

Eight-twelve.

The door opens. Just a few boisterous regulars.

Some say that time heals everything, but I can't agree. It merely waters down the despair until it becomes something else, a derivative weight that sits heavily in the stomach before relocating to the heart. Time certainly blunts the edges if you allow it, which I don't.

Grief is a natural process. If I had a year for each time someone told me that, I'd be immortal. Funny how anguish elicits such benign sentiment, such awkward cliché: *Can't change what's gone. There's a reason for everything. Have to move on. Got to look forward.* Why?

My father would have understood. 'Just look at the stars,' he once told me. I'd opened the telescope that was a badly-kept secret one birthday. 'That's looking back in time.'

I didn't understand then, how the light takes so long to arrive. That if a giant hand could grab a distant star, how it would be ages before we saw it had gone. How if the sun suddenly burned out, we wouldn't know for eight minutes. Four hundred and eighty seconds when the sun wouldn't exist, but we'd still see it. I like that. I think.

Eight-thirteen.

Another wave of guilt flushes through me. This is too soon. Disrespectful. One year is no time at all. I shouldn't be here. I feel a fake. *You have to get out there again, start seeing other people. It's not healthy.* Perhaps she won't turn up. And then I can tell them all that I tried. That I was right to stay at home, keep my head in the sand. Keep it there for another year. And another.

I used to fantasize about stopping time, suspending its inexorable march. We'd be lying in a meadow in summer, nature's chords resounding about us, warmth reaching our faces at the end of its ninety-three-million-mile journey. She'd tell me the Latin name of every wild flower we saw and I'd forget them straight away. I used to think she made up their common names. *Stop teasing*, I'd say as she pointed out Herb Robert, Bird's-foot-trefoil, Ivy-leaved Toadflax and Germander Speedwell. It was only afterwards, when the teasing had stopped forever, that I found her scrapbook under the bed. They were all in there, pressed and labelled, the places we'd picked them. A few had a crude smiley face drawn next to them, but I could never work out what it meant. If I could have frozen the action it would have been on one of those days, walking through golden fields, fields of barley, as the song says. Press the button on the stopwatch, arrest the mechanism, remain there forever.

It gets harder, but if I close my eyes and strain I can still recall her face as it smiles and laughs. The image becomes a little grainier each month—the only clear ones now are from photographs in the box that I'm supposed to be weaning myself off. I'm petrified of the day when recall brings nothing.

Isn't there a theory of infinite universes? Where every conceivable version plays out. Is that linked to the one where all pasts, presents and futures co-exist in alternative realities? So somewhere, in a parallel universe, on a planet the same as this, she is still alive, the shadow on an X-ray absent. No wheezing, no hacking up blood. No interminable stays in hospital, no scarves where curls the colour of obsidian once tumbled from. Is that actually happening somewhere now? Is there comfort to be found in that? I'm not sure, as then there would be a world where we didn't meet. And worlds where she's with someone else. Worlds I cease to exist in. A world where it's to me someone behind a desk delivers an explanation of how passive smoking can cause the word I still can't bring myself to say. (I also find the word passive absurd.) There'd be a planet ten minutes ahead of this, where I'm either fumbling around in the small talk of a first date or finishing my drink alone.

Eight-fourteen.

I look around the bar at the pockets of joy purging the week, leaving it behind in offices, factories, call centres. In the corner an old man sits alone, face creased, eyes vacant—a warning from my future. He gulps from a pint that resembles tar and as it slips into him I imagine it coursing through his veins, buffeting the memories, gorging itself on what's left of his soul. He watches the pub, his pub, ebb character as the young bring lustrous chrome and sofas in with them. He winces as someone drops a pound in the jukebox, taps the screen. I suspect he wants a Tambourine Man, but this jukebox deals mostly in discordant bass: a deluge of noise devoid of melody.

Beside him a sign reminds the man, whilst mocking me, that smoking is now banned inside. As his gnarled yellow fingers roll a moistened Rizla, we share a glance and I wonder if I hate him. Whether I resent the age he's reached. If any of his smoke entered her lungs. He disappears outside.

Eight-fifteen.

I'm tired of chasing time, trying to catch it, prevent it falling through my fingers. I hate how nothing is live, that everything is delayed. At the end, when Jane spoke, I even resented the lapse between her uttering words and me hearing them. It was imperceptible, but as they travelled to my ears and were then processed by my brain, I was always a fraction behind her. Nothing in real time.

Six months, maybe more, the people who know said, as if what we had left could be reduced to units. But later that evening, even I broke it down into hours and it still felt like theft. Minutes seemed more copious, but what can you do in a minute? Almost nothing, I thought at first. I became obsessed with trying to stretch sixty seconds, fill them to the brim, cling to time's relativity. Seventy heartbeats, eight breaths. Two hundred and fifty babies enter the world. The Earth travels eleven hundred miles along its orbit, being struck by six thousand bolts of lightening. All in one tiny minute. And couldn't that minute be halved, and halved again indefinitely? Something to be said for units, after all. There was a sense of power in choosing my own statistics over the ones they'd offered me.

Eight-nineteen.

Half a pint left. I must look ridiculous sat here alone, waiting. Might as well have a sign around my neck. At least the old man is back, the expelled molecules of polonium and arsenic and cadmium and carbon monoxide dispersing safely into the night air. Two men sitting alone, sharing nothing but a moment. I assume he knows tragedy, it's just that he doesn't know mine and the role his kind played in it. Suddenly, I want to tell him. To ask him if he thinks it's fair. I want to shake him, feel my grip around his throat until he begs for her forgiveness. But I don't. The fight is leaving me, the glue that binds one moment to the next implacable. He sees me staring and offers a half smile, which I almost return.

Eight-twenty.

Why am I doing this to myself? Just drink up and slink home to the photographs and empty anniversaries. It was foolish to plan plans.

Between a group of animated men I see a woman walk in. I know it's her. I watch her scan the room, the men scanning her. I could still leave out the back. She buys a drink, fumbles with her purse. It's not too late to go, to risk nothing, but there's something about the way she nervously tucks a curl behind her ear that makes me stay. Again my eyes find the old man's. There's a glint in them now, as if he's present at the start of something. I want to say to him that a start implies an end; love is no less a cycle than the moon and the tide. *It's okay*, he seems to say and I observe the moment as if from above, for the first time glimpsing a time ahead of this one. I once read that if you forced yourself to stare at the sun for eight seconds, you'd go blind. I stand, wave to the woman and smile.

Meet Malcolm

THIRTY-THREE.

He's so fat, the men lowering him have beads of sweat breaking out on their foreheads, despite the cool wind. There are more people here than I'd have thought; a few are tearful. They'll be family: yes, the same corpulent gait. Even the women have the distended cheeks and monobrow. My parents look on earnestly, dutiful if not upset. He did lots for the community . . . their respectful mantra. I'm not normally one for goodbyes, but I couldn't miss this one.

NINE.

I always walk home from school this way now — ever since Mum and Dad had to see the headmaster cos I kept losing my dinner money and coming home with rips in my uniform and blood down my shirt. Me and Chris come this way, even though it's longer, cos we don't have to go past the kids in the year above who always hang out by the park. We usually stop at Uncle Malcolm's house, even though he's not an uncle. He lets us play with his dog and gives us lemonade and those biscuits that you scrape the chocolate off with your top teeth.

THIRTY-THREE.

I check on Rachel and the children. Her to see that she's still deep in slumber, them to remind myself why I'm doing this. Jack is scrunched up in the corner of the top bunk, all wild hair and flushed cheeks, as if he fell asleep mid-play. Below, Sophie is nestled among bears and dolls, more peaceful than her brother yet not as heavily asleep. Outside I go in the shed and change into the clothes I put there yesterday, before slipping out of the back gate. I curse that the night is so clear, but it's unlikely my resolve will remain if I return to the soft *S* of my wife's body. There's a route that goes around the cornfields and along the canal. It takes me about an hour to reach the house.

NINE.

Chris has chicken pox, so I have to walk on my own today and when I get to Uncle Malcolm's, Huckleberry comes running out doing his angry yapping, which would scare some people, but then he just rolls over and lets me rub his tummy and his eyes go all funny like he's in a trance. Uncle Malcolm usually comes out about now, but I can't see him. His door is open so I go inside. There are beer cans on the floor and the smell is like dirty washing and old carpet. There are some toys that look too big for Huckleberry and the curtains are all drawn. I go past the kitchen and see that Uncle Malcolm hasn't washed up for a long time. I can see a flickering light coming from the room at the end of the hall. In the front room the TV is on, and it's strange cos I'm on the screen. Me and Chris, running around the garden chasing Huckleberry. On the sofa Uncle Malcolm is lying there with his shirt undone and his trousers and pants pulled down. He sees me after a while and with his free hand waves me to come over. I run home, falling over on the way, which gets blood on my shirt and Dad asks if I walked home by the park again.

THIRTY-THREE.

I thought of bringing a knife upstairs, but when I wake him and our eyes meet, I know I don't need one. Back in the kitchen, I dictate the letter for him. His handwriting, I notice, is like a child's.

I tell him which way to drive. We pass the occasional homeward drunk along the route. I know how to avoid the streets with cameras and soon we're on country lanes, just a few miles away.

'Where are we going?' he stutters. I let his words hang in the night air as if they were rhetorical.

We're almost there. He stops the car once he realises the road we're on.

'Look, I'm sorry. Please.'

I consider his words and say them to myself. *Sorry. Please.*

'Drive,' I say.

NINE.

Chris's chicken pox got so bad he had to move away. Didn't even see him before he went. Mum and Dad say his parents were atheists, but I don't know what that means or why it made them move away. I do miss him cos I don't have many friends. Uncle Malcolm misses him too and says he's glad we're still friends. He says it's fine to call him Malcolm cos he knows my Mum and Dad from church. I don't want him to feel bad that I ran away that day, so I tell him about the bullies at school and he says they can't get me here. We play on his computer, but he's no good at any of the games cos his fingers are so fat. School finishes next week and I ask him if I can still come round in the holidays.

THIRTY-THREE.

The viaduct is bathed in blue light from the low harvest moon. I tell him to turn the engine off and get out the car. Standing there I realise how ridiculous I must look in my ill-fitting clothes, all bought from charity shops in town this week. The surgeons' gloves and baseball cap complete the absurd look. All of it will be ash by morning.

'It was so long ago,' he says, dropping to his knees. 'You probably don't remember it properly.'

I consider two things: how obese he's become, and the height of the wall.

'You're going to have to jump,' I say.

Homecoming

SHOP FAÇADES OFFERED different wares, but it was the buildings themselves, the roads and trees, that resonated so profusely with a childhood echoing through the decades. And the bridge, of course. He'd crossed it that day, just ahead of the others—breathless, still convinced that some game had gone wrong.

Heading out of the other side of town, there was the river to his left that he'd forgotten. He and a few friends—other friends—used to coax brown trout with the oddest of baits—banana skin, cheddar, sweetcorn—until evolution taught the fish there the perils of things yellow. A life before that August day revealed itself; a childhood that had been erased—a boy that had been forgotten.

Droplets of rain fell regularly from his nose, the occasional one clinging to his septum before running into the groove between his lips. His clothes were sodden now, the wind pressing cold trousers to the front and sides of his legs. The skin on his hands was soft and crinkled; his hair felt like a wet rag had been slapped onto his scalp.

He walked on, drawn out of town like a Hamlin rat. It seemed further than he remembered and Michael wondered if he'd passed the gate already. Perhaps it wasn't there anymore; perhaps it was imagined. He was happy that only one car had passed him.

And then there it was, the same gate, as far as he could

tell. The one that he'd leapt over, barely even touching on that hottest of summer days.

His body reacted to the provocation: his heart danced a little jig—the missed beat of anxiety; his legs telling his brain (or was it the other way around?) that he was on a ship in high seas.

A glance both ways along the road and he slipped through the opening and began to climb the hill. Within a few minutes the land looked alien. He paused and turned full circle, trying to picture the route he'd taken that day in reverse. He altered course a few degrees, quickened his pace.

Flash. A scene. The boy. It almost knocked him off his feet. There'd been no visual flashbacks since the first few years in the unit. And then a long forgotten taste, an acrid tang at the back of his throat. He couldn't place it to anything physical—not smoke or pollen—just the brain eliciting a chemical reaction that was somehow linked to then. He retched a couple of times. This was to be expected; the mutinying of the mind through its shell. You could control thoughts with enough practice, but they would just manifest somewhere else.

Focus on the walking: one, two, three, four.

He turned to see his progress. The town could be covered by a hand. Was it the same hand, though? He scoured its detail. Didn't cells constantly die, being replaced by new ones? Aren't we, literally speaking, recycled every couple of years or so? And without a soul, wasn't it the case that he was no more connected to the boy he was that day than to the ground he now stood on? Only history linked him. Just a narrative, that's all.

Within a minute of setting off again, he realised he was in the field. For a moment he'd fantasized about none of it existing, that there'd been some huge mistake—a conspiracy on a par with faked moon landings and grassy knowls. But it was exactly as he remembered. He'd even entered it from the opening they'd fled through that day.

Despite the rain easing, the ground remained soft underfoot, almost causing his shoes to leave his feet, as if the ground were claiming him. Another flash: the boy freewheeling on his bike down the far side of the field, his concentration in avoiding any bumps or holes keeping the gang from his attention.

Michael suddenly remembered the bike itself; a chunky maroon frame with a ripped saddle. The tyres were a thick grubby white, the spokes all rusted. The handlebars had only one brake and a bell that had chimed as the bike fell over and flipped two whole rolls.

The boy had cried out more in surprise than anything, his voice then dulled as he hit the ground and recoiled. He sprang to his feet like a jack-in-the-box, eyes wide, taking in his aggressors and calculating potential escape routes. There weren't any, of course. Rob Perry was the fastest kid in school; no one had beaten him over a hundred metres since they had started as five-year-olds.

The boy had tried to run, abandoning his bike, making for the hill he'd just descended. Everyone charged after him. Rob got to him first, performing a high rugby tackle, which was effective if not graceful.

Michael paused. Aspects of the account seemed novel to his memory.

They'd surrounded him, watching as, like a felled gazelle, he offered no resistance.

'D'ya know who we are?' someone had said, before questions were turned inward. 'Shall we sort him out, boys?'

'Reckon the little twat's loaded.'

'Who wants to search him?' and then . . . what, exactly?

Michael tried to clear the clutter from his mind, tried to find the version that had become the truth.

They had grabbed him, prompting brief resistance as legs flailed upwards like some upturned beetle.

Michael looked for the route they'd taken to the cricket pavilion that day. So far, today's only destination had been this field, but now the urge to see where the building had been overwhelmed him. He turned to his right and set off to the opposite corner.

The boy was held by each arm, with Shaun leading them. Michael and another—he couldn't remember who—brought up the rear. He was certain he hadn't held the boy. Certain.

Sure enough, the gap in the hedge that wasn't quite a gateway was still there, and within a minute or two, Michael was looking at the spot where the fire had been. For years he'd obsessed about what, if anything, would be in this exact place: some sort of memorial, a new building . . . or just revived ground.

He could see something, not a building, but something man-made.

The object was a bench. It faced out from the edge of the field back towards the town. Did he want to go farther? There would be some words on it. Did he need to punish himself anymore today?

He remembered that the boy hadn't uttered a word; that he'd quickly accepted both the status of prisoner and the futility of escape, and walked compliantly on. There had also been no dialogue between the gang, their movements seemingly subject to the person in front or to the side, like a flock of starlings.

They'd lit about three fires already that day—all of which had threatened to spread beyond control. Watching each one grow before swatting the flames with T-shirts became a test of nerve.

Animals, too, were fair game. They would place whatever had been found—insects, an adder—in an empty paint tin with a few dry leaves, before holding a magnifying glass between the contents and the sun. They had matches, but this way the heat spot could be directed perfectly. Most just shrivelled as they ignited, some crackled and hissed as fluid and small bones were heated. Some seemed to whine, screech almost, flinging themselves around the curvature of their metallic crematorium.

They found exhilaration turned to anti-climax with the death of the creatures. This was even more pronounced when each subsequent one proved no bigger than the last. Each extinction raised the stakes for the next.

As they drifted from field to field, they had boasted elaborate plans to trap bigger prey over the remainder of the holidays. There was talk of food-filled boxes to entice rodents, poisoned meat in trees to incapacitate but not kill birds. Shaun, needing to outdo everyone, talked of hunting rabbits at dawn with his father in the very same fields only days before.

When they reached the old cricket pavilion, there was a loss of momentum, as no one seemed quite sure what should happen next. For a moment as they all stood around, looking at each other, the day stood still. The fields around them seemed as big as the world could be. There was little wind and not the slightest noise. You could look in every direction and see no movement, save a lone buzzard hovering high in the thermals, scanning for food, oblivious to gratuitous violence.

Michael forced himself to approach the bench; the ground yielded more, as if protecting it.

'What you doing in our field?' Shaun said. The boy kept his chin to his chest.

'You have to pay fifty pence to come through here,' said Rob with less conviction. Still nothing.

From nowhere, the stalemate was broken as someone shoved the boy hard to the floor. Again, they seemed to act without reference, marching him into the building through the back door they'd forced open earlier.

The boy was sniffling now. What should have sparked sympathy just made some of them angry. Shaun disappeared, before returning with his T-shirt covering his head and most of his face. They all started chanting, the noise driving them on. Someone brought in a length of rope. Who? He tried to sharpen the image. The boy was tied, his arms horizontal, to two wooden uprights—Michael only now picturing a crucifixion. The motion seemed unstoppable. Rubbish was placed around the boy like kindling. Then the dares began. *Go on. I did the last one. It's your turn.* They just wanted to scare him.

Near the end of his time in the secure unit, Michael had requested several medical and forensic books, spending hours buried in them, building up knowledge of what would have happened once they left the boy.

The fire would have spread quickly, the dry wood of the old building proving the perfect fuel. Noxious gases from the thermal degradation of the wood probably didn't reach lethal levels by themselves, tending to incapacitate instead. At its most intense, the fire would have reached up to five hundred degrees centigrade, the air around the flames causing burns to the face, mouth and nasal passages. It was possible that the boy's larynx convulsed sufficiently to cause suffocation, or that the hot air led to reflex cardiac death. The most likely cause of death, though, would have been through smoke inhalation, which would have caused hypoxia as the oxygen levels remained high enough to allow combustion, but not life.

When found, the blackened torso would have assumed a pugilistic posture, its limbs flexed and rigid. As tissue lost its moisture and bones fractured, the body would have become several inches shorter, as well as losing up to sixty percent of its weight. There would have been splits in the skin of the limbs and abdomen as it contracted in the heat, losing all its elasticity. Evidence that the boy was alive during the fire would have come from soot particles found below his vocal chords. Depending on how long it took the firemen to extinguish the blaze (Michael had avoided the television coverage as much as possible), identity of the body could have been difficult, perhaps requiring dental records or historical orthopaedic clues.

The rain was heavy again, cleansing the earth around him. Twenty years of trying to forget had chipped away at the truth. He was still sure he'd only stood there, more an observer, watching evil unfurl, helpless to stop it. Sure as you can be.

Michael looked at the lustrous plaque on the bench: *In loving memory of Andrew Wilkinson, Aged 9. Your spirit will always shine.*

Hare's Running

IT'S ALL GOING *to shit and we're going to get caught!* Matt's shouting at the cars in front, banging the horn, telling me to drive faster, to use the pavement if I have to, telling me the other way would have been quicker, that it's all my fault, that he knew I'd fuck it up, our one chance to get out of this sorry bastard of a town.

To be fair to Matt, he lived on his nerves, which in turn lived on caffeine, Old Holburn, single malts, Red Bull and amphetamines. Life, it was easy to imagine, was wonderfully uncomplicated for him, measured entirely in chemical and financial highs and lows.

I knew almost nothing else about him; anything else wasn't for public consumption, as far as I could tell. You only got to see the façade of people like Matt. In the eight months I'd known him, he'd worn three subtly different pastel shirts, two pairs of ill-fitting jeans and the same scuffed Caterpillar boots. A tan leather jacket that looked as if it'd never been new completed the ensemble. His copious black hair was always slicked back so that it resembled a bird caught in an oil spill. In contrast, his skin was wan, almost ghostly (outdoors was for other people, he would say), and his face seemed always to wear three days' stubble—never more, never less.

When I met him, he was running the pub round the corner from the snooker hall I work in. (I get minimum wage and fifty percent off one of the less popular lagers.)

He would drift in for a last one once he'd locked up and we'd bitch about the parochial denizens we found ourselves among, how if you didn't get out of this place by thirty-five, you never would. We'd sometimes play pool till it got light, sleep all day, then head to work as most people went home. A few weeks of this and Matt's purpose in life began to reveal itself.

One night, whilst doing the till, I noticed his eyes gleamed with more than the usual narcotic lustre. His brain was scheming. The distraction was welcome in what had been a shitty week. I was supposed to be looking after my mother's cat while she sunned herself in Tenerife with her latest toy boy, but the stupid thing was petrified in my flat. First chance it got, it bolted out the door into the street and straight under the number forty-three, which for once was on time. The trip to the vet's was superfluous, but they boasted a number of options for disposal, one of which included freezing Merlin for six days so Mum could say goodbye properly when she returned. They'd patch him up, stick him in their icebox, and as long as I gave them a few hours' notice, they could thaw him in time for the teary send off. Seemed the least I could do.

'Only 30p out,' I said to Matt as I compared the cash to the till receipt.

'Yeah, but this place only takes five quid a day. What's your tab like?'

'Don't ask.'

'Don't ask, don't get.' And with that he took out an impressive looking bunch of keys, placing them ceremoniously on the bar.

And that's how it started. I gave it a moment's thought, however long a moment is, but I owed the till nearly two hundred quid, most of which I'd shovelled into the fruit machine during the dull afternoon hours. I checked the doors again, pulled another two pints and watched as he tried to open the bottom door of Big Deal.

'Bollocks,' he said. 'Let's try the back.' He pulled it away from the wall and disappeared. Then, as if by magic, pound coins began to fill the tray; each click Matt made yielded another. I put a beer cloth beneath the stream to stifle the noise. Within a few minutes the tray was full. I started to pile the money on the bar.

'Not done yet,' he said.

'Eh?'

'You can't just empty the tubes, there'll be nothing to pay out if a jackpot rolls in tomorrow. We have to play it, get a big win, so it doesn't chuck any out for a while.'

And so we did, pulled up two stools, a third for the ashtray and began putting the coins back in. Every time we won something Matt would gamble it away, losing ten, twenty, fifty quid. 'Gotta go all the way, mate.'

Finally, around 4 a.m., there were enough nudges for four bells and a hundred and fifty quid. Matt necked his pint, rolled a fag and found a comfy chair to survey his work. 'Drinks on you, I reckon,' he said.

We would hang out together most days, drifting around the pubs and cafes and bookies till our shifts started.

John Dylan Bookmakers was as tawdry and unwelcoming within its walls as was suggested by its grimy façade. It had so far resisted the corporate upgrading of its contemporaries, instead keeping faith with the more traditional, gnarled punter: yellow fingered, dandruff-spattered donkey jacket, battle-hardened eyes that told you not to ask how lady luck was treating them. Asking a true gambler how their day was going was like asking a cancer patient how their disease was progressing, unless of course they were winning.

There was an unfathomable stench to the place, a unique blend of cheap coffee, wheeling smoke, old and new sweat, and fear. Beneath the discarded, screwed up betting slips, the carpet tiles, once a chequered pattern, were now a homogenous treacle colour. The TV screens were grainy, not from weak reception, but years of encrusted silt. Often during a race they would flicker and ping off as if in protest.

Men scoured the jaundicing racing pages stuck to the walls, hoping a lifelong thus-far-failed formula was going to have its day. Tension would swell as the horses entered their stalls. Odds nudged up or down a point or two. Last minute bargains were sought. Rumours fizzed round the room. *Going down. They're off.* Then silence, all eyes and ears to the screens. The occasional whisper between regulars. You never knew what had been backed, the quiet only broken when a horse emerged from the pack, followed by a *Get on!* and you realised you'd blown your money. Curses cut the air. Then the tension flat-lined—back to studying the walls, back to scheming and scurrying.

'We're gonna do the dogs,' announced Matt.

'You can't beat the system. Everything's been tried.'

And we had tried in the short time we'd known each other. There were little tricks, sleight of hand and nuance that could give you an edge. Half the battle with dogs is whether they get out their traps ahead of the others. You can have a short favourite, but if it's behind or gets knocked coming out, forget it. So when the slowest of the staff were on, we'd find a fancied greyhound, write out a slip for two quid and hover at the back of the queue of last minute bets. *Hare's running.* Patience. Hold your fire. Pretending you want the woman to hurry up as you've already written your slip, whilst holding back is an art.

She sees you've written it, sees the anguish in your eyes that you might miss the race, but has to serve others first. Then they're off. If our dog doesn't get out cleanly we hand it over as it is. If it does, one of us distracts her, whilst the other, unseen, adds a zero to the two before handing it over. It's just about an edge. Tipping things in your favour. Sometimes we'd leave the trap number blank till the last minute instead. Worked for a while, till they got smart to it.

'You can't beat the bookies, Matt.'

'That's why I joined them.'

John Dylan had a second, smaller shop in a village a few miles away, a small premises with just a counter and a till for the locals who couldn't get to town. This was where Matt now worked two days a week. The shop was only open from ten till one, time for people to put their bets on, go home and watch the racing, collect any winnings the next day. Matt would bag up the takings and betting slips, drive back to Dylan's and hand it in.

'It's easy,' he said, rummaging through my flat for something to drink. 'You come in, write out a few slips, everything but which trap, I'll put them through the machine so they're timed, but we leave them intact. We lock up, drive to mine like maniacs in time for two races at a lunchtime meet, check the results on Teletext and write the winners on the slip. I tear off your half for you, go to the shop and you come in to collect the next day. Quids in.

'Aren't they all photographed these days? The slips.'

'Old man Dylan's too tight to splash out in his small place. They're just stamped with the date and amount, like in the old days.'

And so we tried it. Just a few quid, nothing to raise

eyebrows: mostly wins, a couple of forecasts. I'd collect the money in the village where Matt would give me a wink across the counter.

'He'll spot something soon, ya know,' I said one night in the club.

'I know. He's already asking about the lucky bastard in the village.'

'We should call it a day.'

'What about hitting him big?'

'What's the point getting greedy? Just draw more attention.'

'I mean really big, a one off, then quit.'

'What's really big?'

'I dunno, a grand, an Archer.'

'Fuck's an Archer?'

'Keep up, mate. Two grand. Jeffrey. Prostitute. Envelope full of cash . . .'

'Never work.'

'Why not?'

And although I could think of several reasons, some part of me opted for silence and its implied complicity.

'We're not gonna fucking make it. Put your foot down.'

Old man Dylan expected Matt no later than one-fifteen, even with traffic. It wouldn't have mattered, wouldn't have had to be today, but Dylan had let Matt go, told him to finish today, cutbacks and all, but I reckon he smelt something. Didn't matter, said Matt. He'd still have to pay out.

'I told you we should have brought someone else in,' I said. 'They could have texted us the results.'

'Two goes into a thousand more than three.'

We'd decided on one bet. A tricast in the 12:50. A ridiculous bet reserved for lottery players and dreamers.

Even if the shortest priced ones came in, we'd win nine-hundred from a twenty-five-quid bet. Nobody bet that much on a dog in this town, let alone on three in the right order. But like Matt said, what could Dylan do?

My beaten-up Astra slid the last few yards along the pavement outside his block and we were out quicker than the Dukes of Hazzard, taking the stairs four at a time.

I turned the TV on.

'Fuck's the remote?' said Matt as he searched the pile of empty beer cans and take-away cartons that passed for his floor.

'You could have looked for it last night.'

I stared at the TV screen as Fiona Bruce told us that interest rates had stayed the same, that a lorry had overturned on the M4, but not about the 12:50 at Romford.

'Can't you get Teletext up without it?' I said.

'Fuck. Fuck. Fucking fuck.'

Matt ran out the door and I heard him climbing the stairs. Following him seemed to make sense. He banged on a door.

'Chris, you in? CHRIS.' Nothing. Further up. More banging. No answer.

'What'll we do?' I said, as Matt slumped against the door. 'How . . .'

'Shut up, I'm thinking.' With that he tore back down the stairs. 'Come on. Bring that fucking ticket.'

We cut through an alley and several service lanes, ran across the park and into the High Street. As my lungs burned and nausea hit me, it struck me that someone who treats their body like Matt shouldn't be able to run so fast.

We were almost at Dylan's. 'Matt, wait.' Suddenly he darted into Curry's. When I found him, he was remonstrating with one of the staff.

'But I am going to fucking buy it. I want to see the remote.'

'I'm sorry, sir, but we don't have a remote control for that display model.'

'What about that one?'

'I don't think . . .'

'Look, do any of these have a fucking remote you can show me?'

I stood there, hands on knees, gulping what air I could, whilst the man looked around, trying to calculate just how crazy his current customers were. 'Um, the Samsung over there . . .'

Matt ran to it, switched it on and grabbed the remote. Within a few seconds he'd found the page and stood fixated. I walked over to him.

'Fuck me,' he said. 'Look at that.'

I didn't even read the dogs' names, just scanned their odds. 'We can't do it now.'

'Why not?'

'Cos it's . . .' I did the maths, 'about a hundred and fifty to one.'

'Hundred and sixty.'

'That's almost four grand. What happened to the favourites?'

'Who cares? Come on, write it out.'

Other shoppers were staring at us now.

'Got a pen?' I said. Matt's eyes bore into me and a vein rose on his left temple.

The assistant came over. 'I'm afraid . . .'

'If I want assistance, I'll . . . ah, just borrow this.' Matt took the young man's pen from his shirt pocket, grabbed the slip from my hand and rested it on the TV.

'You'll have to leave now, please.'

Outside the shop, Matt pulled the slip apart, handed

me the bottom half and ran off towards Dylan's. I looked at my watch: one-thirty.

The antiseptic reek in the waiting room of the vet's was turning my stomach. We were the only ones without a pet. Owners looked nervously at each other, forcing half smiles, as they clung to their various sized boxes. Mum had insisted we come straight here once I told her.

'They need time, Mum. To let him thaw.'

'Take me to Merlin, now.'

Driving here, I'd pictured the staff tearing around, turning up the heating, considering the microwave. Two hours later, they called us through. There he was, peaceful and content looking, magically reincarnated from the blood-soaked fur ball I'd brought in a week earlier.

'Does he feel warm to you, Ben?' said Mum.

I stroked him. 'Not really,' but it was obvious they'd overdone it with the microwave or whatever.

I led Mum back to the car, promising to bury Merlin in her garden the next day.

'Stop the car,' Mum said, as we pulled away. 'We didn't pay the bill, I have to go back. It must have been a fortune.'

'It's fine, Mum. All taken care of.'

Breathe

I WANT TO SEE if I can breathe in Her presence. This basic yet beautiful function—controlled by the brainstem, regulated according to how much oxygenated blood our muscles call for—it's time to test it again.

In the heart of night the breath is usually cadent, its chaste rhythm like the tide, comforting an anxious parent, annoying a sleepless lover—always there, from the first inhalation after departing the amniotic fluid, to the last exhalation at the far end of life. But not mine.

When we met, I thought I was allergic to Her perfume, that first corporeal connection as the musk caught my single-malt-coated throat. But those times She wore none—after a shower or when it had been adulterated by the more viscous sweat of lovemaking—my intercostals still crushed me like a jacket for the insane.

It takes just shy of an hour to remove my dusty journals and tomes: *Small's Personality and Pulmonary Abnormities*; *Porter's Evidence for the Psychosomatic Origin of Asthma* and several hundred others. The padlock removed, the long box open, I start the timer.

I last a stroke beyond four minutes before the tightening begins. A whole minute more than last year. I look at my wife. Films and colleagues had led me to believe the bones of the skeleton exhaust their lustre with time, so I'm surprised She's lost none of Her inner radiance. The wedding ring has turned around on the proximal phalanx of Her third finger, so carefully I correct it.

I let Her beauty fall on my eyes then wish Her a Happy Birthday.

Offline

'IT CAN'T GO on like this.'

'I'm looking, there's nothing out there.'

'Your father would be ashamed.'

'Stop it, Mum. What time's the funeral?'

'14:30. Don't be late. And make sure you can get a signal.'

This was Mum's way of telling me not to spend all day in Crazy J's. It was about the only place on the planet you couldn't get a signal; that's why people liked it, a sort of nostalgia for a time when you could be offline. Whilst soundproofing the rooms for the live music on Friday nights, someone had cut a corner, used a banned material in the walls, which blocked certain radio waves. They tried to prosecute using the old terror laws, but the court ruled it would be hazardous to remove it and so it remains there today, cocooning its patrons in anonymity. Logging off was illegal, but having no signal wasn't.

J's owner was an old fashioned Turk called Zafer. He was one of the last to be let in before the citizenship exams were made impossible—came here to become a teacher, ended up making a fortune in wind turbines before buying his place.

And today it was the last independent bar in the country. The council had tried to close it several times, but Zafer still had contacts in low places. Last week he was in court for serving alcohol to the under 25s. His defence claimed the group was using fake ID, but prosecutors pointed out he was still connected to the Oracle by cable and should retina-scan every young person as they entered. He got off with a final warning.

A renegade, Zafer was hooked on fare from another age: fried non-organic food, beer that was brewed, which he served if there were no strangers in. He could still get it all, though nobody knew from where. A few years ago, he smuggled tobacco back from China. I'd only ever seen footage of people smoking it on my pod. He rolled it in gummed paper and a few of us tried some. It made me cough and feel light-headed for a bit, but otherwise I couldn't see what the fuss was about. Zafer said his father used to take it forty times a day.

I popped in for an espresso. A few usuals were watching one of Zafer's classic films, the one about a boy who goes away to school to learn magic. There's lots of them; I downloaded one of the ibooks last year, but never read it.

'Hey, Reb.'

'Zaf.'

'You stick around? We play pool later.'

'Can't. Gotta get a job. Mum's gonna kick me out soon.'

'I give you job.'

'I meant a real one.'

Everyone turned around as if I'd blasphemed.

'You bury your grandfather today, no?' said Zafer.

'This afternoon.'

'I liked that man. He was old school. Can you burn me a copy?'

I said that I would.

I walked past the Museum of Consumer Heritage. Mum took me in there when I was young. Everything's just as it was apparently, except the food is all plastic now. You get a trolley, plug your pod in for commentary and push it round the shop just like they used to. Upstairs, above the food, there are the huge old-style computers and TVs on display, clothes that you see in the old films, books with pages. Mum said you could buy everything in the one place—furniture, pets, and of course food. They started having dentists and plastic surgeons on site. People were getting their teeth and noses done in between buying their groceries. Mum said everyone had enough when the bigger ones started cloning their food beneath the stores. Sausages, eggs, bananas—all grown from Petri dishes. Within a few months they didn't need suppliers, just scientists. It was said each store only employed ten or so people who lived underground; everything else was automated. One night a group of organic extremists blew up a store and the backlash started.

MESSAGE INCOMING said my pod. It was my sister boasting the scar from her operation, which I couldn't really make out on the screen. She'd been in for one of those kidney swaps (*To show the special person in your life how much you love them*). The new boyfriend thought it'd be fun. There was a rumour on *GossipVine* that he'd exchanged with someone else years ago, so fuck knows whose my sister had now. Gran said they did it with tattoos in her day. 'Don't forget the funeral,' the message ended.

I thought about Grandad. The only organ rearranging he knew about was when he fought the Taliban at the start of the century. He'd have hated today—all the spectacle of eFunerals. The extra cameras you got in the top package (*For that perfect shot*). He'd have baulked at the small print that said after a year you could only download the bit up to the speeches, making you subscribe again and again. When his Will was posted on the family page, we saw he'd asked for a religious reading, which shocked us all. None of us knew, not even Gran. Kept it to himself, the silly old bastard. We applied to the Committee for Spiritual Exemption to have hymns, but our points total fell just short. We could record anything we wanted over it once we'd subscribed, but it would have been nice on the day.

I checked my tokens to see if I could get the shuttle into the central zone, but my pod told me there was a phase-seven security, so I walked.

The summer rain had lashed down for weeks now, the winter sun a distant memory. High above me, on the side of the disused monorail, news scrolled across. A gang of eco sabs had vandalised the offices of NukeTec again. A woman had been given four hundred hours' civil repayment duty for running her car off one of the old bio-fuels. Riots continued over the fat tax. For a moment I heard Gran's voice saying there was no crime in her day, that people had a sense of morality then.

I reached Optimum Recruitment (*Full Employment and Nothing Less*), my sodden clothes clinging to me as I stood in the SecuriScan. Once cleared, I uploaded my details to a crib and within seconds was staring at a picture of myself, below which were my physical and mental attributes, my sporadic work history, plus current health status and life expectancy. Symbols flashed next to some of my health screening sections, before a voice reminded me of the four-hundred credit fine for not submitting to Disease Projection Analysis. I was missing diabetes and chronic cellular disruption syndrome, among others.

'Do you require a service?' it asked.

'Vacancies,' I said.

'What sector?'

'I was hoping for —'

'The correct response given your profile is *sales*, *maintenance* or *production*.'

'Er, sales.'

'Thank you. Running scan now.'

The screen then advertised weight-loss retreats in space (*Only ten thousand credits if you sign up for three generations*). My sister is saving for one in her perennial quest to become a size minus, not that she'll be able to get her carbon rating down after her trip to see what's left of Amsterdam.

'There are two vacancies you qualify for. Please select one.'

The first was a company called Energization. A squat, balding man took me on a virtual tour through the Com Pod, where, if successful, I would help energise the lives of up to three hundred people a month. 'Come join the harmony,' he said, prompting the staff around him to turn and beam at the camera.

'Menu,' I said.

The other job was selling long-life insurance. Grandad always bemoaned the premiums, which doubled each year once you passed ninety.

I felt the will to live ebbing away. Maybe I could work in Zafer's for a while, get Mum off my back. Get this place off my back.

'Menu.'

'Do you wish to be regarded for any vacancy?' it asked.

I disconnected and stuck on a serotonin patch (*For instant joy all day long*). I checked the time — 14:10 — and decided to find a quieter spot for the ceremony.

The only public grass in the southern zone was around the memorial for victims of the great northern tsunami. I was grateful it was empty apart from an old woman reading the list of names from under an umbrella. She saw me putting on my black tie and smiled.

I found the tree with the largest canopy, activated my pod's camera and saw that I was last online. Mum's face was a mixture of relief and disapproval. My sister was draped over her boyfriend in some health bar. Gran was sat up in bed.

The screen flickered to the opening scene of The Other Side's promotional spiel. Doves were perched above the team of white-suited directors, who were managing to look both earnest and sycophantic at once. Maudlin pipe music cut in, before a voice-over told us today's ceremony was kindly sponsored by Nanotech (*Small is Big*).

An anaemic-looking woman in a black silk kimono guided us through the main hall and into the Peace and Processing room, where Grandad lay on a quilted pyre, festooned with lilies and logos. It went quiet and she read out his name, said how he'd fought for his country, that he was a wonderful family man, before her gaze rolled skyward in solemnity.

We were then all introduced. Gran spoke first, as the director cut to a close-up of her face.

She talked about the brave man she knew, his kindness, how he laughed at everything, how he never compromised his values. I had no idea he'd been part of the '20s' revolt. Gran's thirty seconds remaining bleep sounded, which seemed to throw her into confusion, and the countdown on the screen just ran down in silence. Mum mentioned the beach holidays he took them on when she was a child, how he was there for her when Dad died in the third oil war. When it got to my sister, she was blubbering too much to say anything, so her boyfriend said that although he'd never met him, he was sure Grandad was great.

And then the screen cut to me. I hadn't planned anything. At Dad's I'd been too young to speak, not that there was much left of him to address. Mum had read out the email from the army, which explained that as a new recruit Dad wasn't entitled to a Mac Shield Suit that would have saved him, but her words were edited out before we were granted copyright.

As I stuttered away, the director increased the music and zoomed in on Grandad's ashen face, before cutting to each family member in turn. I could see Mum starting to panic that I wasn't going to say anything, knowing I'd not want to record over it later.

I thought about the last time I spoke to Grandad, when he told me not to fret about getting a job, that I should try to see what was left of the world before it disappeared. As he lay dying in the transition ward, he told me about a remote island in the Pacific that he'd taken Gran to before they were married. Later, I searched the net and the live pictures showed water levels hadn't consumed it yet. I couldn't bring myself to tell him I'd never have the credits to get there, but a short sentence in his Will reminded me that Grandad always had the last word.

I looked across through the rain to the old woman who was placing a single white rose at the base of the barbed fence that protected the marble wall from graffiti. I remember thinking as a child how the names seemed to stretch up forever and how I couldn't read the top few lines.

Thirty seconds remaining . . . the screen said.

My sister had stopped crying. 'Reb!' she said. 'Say something.'

Twenty seconds.

The display split into two: a different angle of Grandad one side, me the other. The edges of the screen had been softened to look like clouds. The camera zoomed in on my image until only my eyes could be seen. I could almost hear the producer shouting for a tear.

Ten seconds.

'Reb.'

I looked at Grandad's face, but all I could see was him as a young man on that island, sand between his toes, running around the woman he loved. I thought of Zafer calling him old school and how I hoped someone would say the same about me one day.

Five. Four. Three. Two.

What was there to say? I logged off.

One Story

I'M HAULED IN from a lascivious daydream by Bach. Not with clean, soothing harmonics, but the tinny, waspish noise of my vibrating mobile. Bach was supposed to rankle less than the shop setting, but context is the decisive factor and it may as well be fingernails rasping across a blackboard. The small screen says Carol is calling. Again. I guiltily tap my keyboard so there's less blank page: *kna dfiu,ssi hfis usnsr.* Not exactly the *magnum opus* I've promised her for the last two months, but I find some small comfort in the inane characters. A few more notes and it'll go to answer-phone. I'll listen to the message later, once the gin has soaked in. Her words will be coldly encouraging, with a less than subtle nod to deadlines come and gone.

I'd tell her you can't get blood from a reluctant stone, were it not a cliché. Something fresh then, about how extracting any more words from me for this collection will be like ringing water from a sponge that's been months in the desert. Jesus. This is the calibre of sentence I'm capable of at present. To think how I sneer when one of my post-grads asks me what to do about writer's block. I tell them that it's a synonym for apathy, an allusion to indifference, that there just is no excuse. Writing's not an art (they hang on every syllable, bless them) where inspiration flows ethereally into you. It's a craft. It's graft. You have to bleed and sweat and cry, and when you do, the words will come. At least, they have until now.

Of course, I believe none of this; I'm more of the *If it doesn't come like leaves to a tree, it probably shouldn't come at all . . .* but you can't very well inform an entire creative writing group that their collective cup of talent is in no danger of brimming over. You have to look for the positives, whether they exist or not, else you'd despair. So far, I've seen little sign of original thought. Even the delightful Jess, who has so far resisted all offers of private tuition, trots out formulaic drivel fit for some tawdry monthly that tells its readers they're all fallow literary greats. Who was it that said there's a book in everyone, and for most that's where it should stay? And when did the creation of fiction become just another career path to choose? It's supposed to choose you. I mean, can you imagine everyone wanting to be a neurosurgeon just because it's featured on some trashy daytime TV show? Second-rate degree courses spreading like Chlamydia, any feckless scribbler who's appeared in some god-awful anthology calling themselves a writer. No, if Jess's pants aren't floor-bound soon, she'll start getting more germane marks.

I swill my glass around, seeing if the ice elicits any more gin from the lemon. It doesn't. The thing I miss most about marriage is its nuance, its sense of habit. B would hear the clink of ice and top me up, not a word from either of us. In the end, I think we both found conversation to be over-rated.

The kitchen is dark and cold. The tonic's lower than I thought, so I go half and half. The house has the welcome feel of a vacuum tonight, hermetically sealed from the stench of reality; my only clue to the comings and goings of the children since their mother's *This-is-what-your-father's-done-this-time* farewell speech, has been the slamming of doors. Still, I find the petulance and silence of adolescence preferable to a heart to heart with a daughter on the verge of coming out and a son who thinks protesting can save the world. They'll toddle off to live with B when she summons them, when Daddy's found her somewhere in the suburbs. I sit back down and consider taking up smoking again.

Here we go. One last story to finish this collection. Not that I see why nine stories aren't enough. Can you imagine Dylan or Bowie being told the album needs another song to finish it off? Fucking Carol. Ten is such a better number, more balanced. She only sees product. Sales. Marketability and other made-up words.

Where was I? A beginning. Just one true sentence to lead the way. That's what Hemingway did when he fretted. Reckoned he could relax then. I look at the blinking cursor and the word cursing comes to mind. Just write something, see what comes out. Remember: the first draft of anything is shit. I can think of a few last drafts as well.

I'm not suited to the short form; it's too precise. Too gimmicky. I don't like compression. Should never have agreed to it. Wouldn't be doing it if people had the fucking time to read a novel these days. I'd proposed something with gravitas, an epic, an old fashioned *tour de force*—my *Midnight's Children*, my prize-winner. 'Everyone's going short these days,' Carol said. 'How about a collection?' I suppose the Booker will be novellas-only before long.

Perhaps a little online poker. Fifty quid, no more. See if that bastard who bluffed me off the table last week is around. Just one game, another drink and I'll be ready.

Fuck.

Who hits a full house on the river twice in a row? Lucky prick. Probably some lank teenager holed up in his airless bedroom in Idaho, with nothing better to do than calculate odds and masturbate.

Back to it.

I could mark something from this week's workshop, elevate my ego with violent strikes of red ink and pejorative scrawls in the margins. Could smell Jess's for any lingering fragrance. (I love the ambiguity in that sentence.)

No, stop procrastinating. Start.

Fucking beginnings. Who did they say didn't do beginnings or ends, just middles? One of the Russians, I think. Or maybe Joyce.

Start with basics. Got to draw the reader in, preferably with a cold hard slap to the face. Grab their throats. Let them know whose story it is, how it's going to be told, when and where, usual shit. Need a voice they can trust to take them on a journey uninterrupted by doubts over reliability, or fears they're being duped. You can't espouse naturalism and suddenly toss in some magical realism to suit your denouement. That's cheating. They don't like it. If you're going to be unreliable, they need to know straight away, which is more or less what B said as she packed. It's fine to hold back. Let them wander helplessly in unfamiliar terrain, toss them a sign here and there, but you can't pull the rug from under them anymore. People love to see what's coming, but only once it's come, if that makes sense.

Could concentrate on style. Something playful that daisy chains from one character or event to another, all cleverly linking back to the first. All effect over substance. Seems *en vogue*. Make the first narrator a virus or a garden gate or a grain of sand. No, no.

Start with character, yes, that's always worked. One long gulp for lucidity, a top-up, then look for material to draw on. Usually start in my personal life, but that's been plundered enough for this collection. Not that you can avoid it entirely; your primordial swamp will always seep through, they say. They?

Brainstorm. See what comes.

A child who grows up on a farm so that her first words are all onomatopoeic. *Moo, Baa. Oink.*

A malevolent dentist who drills deeper than he needs.

A woman who can only talk in song lyrics.

A man who loses things. A wife. His children's respect. The ability to construct a sentence.

The computer, as if sensing the egregious bullet points, grinds to a halt. Freezes under the strain of long periods of inactivity followed by typing. The anti-virus balloon appears, claiming the computer may be at risk, which I can't disagree with.

Instead of thrusting a fist into the monitor, I turn to the day job. I find Jess's piece half way down the pile. Smells of paper, nothing more. I wade through the first paragraph, which is laden with political angst. It has the subtlety of a wrecking ball—I'd guessed it was set in Guantanamo from the title. Three pages in and I'm beaten into submission by prose so purple it induces nausea. I place 'Orange is not the Only Suit' back with the others and head to the kitchen for a refill. The mound of ready-meal packaging has gained height, suggesting my offspring have eaten before seeking whatever brand of hedonism is flavour of the month in town.

A conversation still lingers above the dining room table, despite being a month old.

'You've never cared about any of the others,' I'd said.

'They were all young,' said B.

'I thought that would be worse.'

'So did I.'

This one's nearly all gin, but still barely touches the sides.

I deem some sort of cigarette to be necessary and head upstairs. My son's room, I realise as my head peers in, is out of bounds. I'm sure he finds the clutter homely, but I'd want some protective clothing to enter. My daughter's room, the place she occasionally spends the hours between 4 a.m. and midday in, is tidier, almost clinical. I'm drunk enough to discard any issues of privacy; I pay the mortgage, I tell myself, rummaging through drawers and boxes. Nothing. Various Rizla packets—I'd have welcomed the challenge to roll my own—but there's no sign of tobacco. A 2008 diary tempts me for a second, perhaps for material, but they say you get what you deserve when you read someone's journal, and I can do without the contempt. A photograph of B is stuck on the bottom corner of the dressing table mirror. I scan the rest of the room, but it's the only one. Always the mummy's girl.

I give up, close the door behind me. As I stumble down the stairs, more ghostly conversations follow me.

'You'll never change.'

'Some would regard that a virtue.'

'Now there's a word I don't associate with you these days.'

'Come on, B. You can't expect a man to stick his cock in the same hole for the rest of his life. It's fanciful. Genetic folly.'

'I'd forgotten how charming you could be.'

Weighing up the risk of driving, I suddenly remember an unopened box of cigars, a gift from my agent after finishing my first and only novel three years ago. What did that cretinous little man say about *The Renegade Diaries* in his broadsheet? *If I had to recommend one book, just one, from all those out there this summer, just one novel not to read, this would be it.* Cheap. Sales were certainly modest, but they targeted the wrong demographic. And then that cunt on the review show called it a techno-thriller with flawed technology and little thrill.

The hand-rolled Bolivar draws a hacking cough as I inhale from habit. Recovered I try to discern some of its flavours, but as with wine, I'm found wanting. B was the one with the refined palate. Good breeding, her father would pronounce, usually with a condemning glance my way. As I picture the old fart, I consider it odd not to have heard from their family solicitor by now, but then remember I've not opened the post for a week.

I ponder the word. Breeding. That wondrous happening with the unfortunate by-product. A daughter who'll presumably be doing none of her own, a son embarking on a career as an eco-warrior; I consider which genes of mine have supposedly shaped them. What paternal pearls of wisdom will they carry with them through life? What aesthetic sensibility will they tell others was my legacy? No, I donated my seed, which in turn contributed to reasonable IQs and a bit of asthma. Any other connection is merely circumstantial.

Back to the dark art of storytelling.

Two noises. One persistent, grating, the other a soft clacking as I move my head. As I lift the side of my face off the keyboard, the answer-machine on the house phone kicks in. It's B. Something about coming round in the morning to collect some stuff. Coming round with Arran, whoever the fuck he is. I can feel the indentations of keys on my face. A haiku on my cheek. I feel like ten kinds of shit.

In the kitchen I abandon dilution and opt for neat gin. It bites my throat on the way down. Couple more and I'll have to start on the wine.

The front door slams. Stairs taken three at a time—son, not daughter. I climb the stairs in serpentine fashion and push open his door.

'The icecaps safe tonight, then, Jack?' I ask.

'Can't stop. Got to be somewhere.'

'Let me guess: knitting bongos outside some landfill?'

'I see you're drunk for a change.'

'When you've lived with your mother a few more years, you'll see it's a perfectly desirable state. Care to join me for one?'

His face looks full of pity. 'One. It's never one.'

I watch him force clothes deep into a rucksack. 'Bit of a holiday?'

'Few days. Week at most.'

'Some sort of demonstration, I suppose?'

'Something like that.'

'And will you be living here on your return?'

'Probably not.'

'So I won't keep a room for you?'

'Up to you.'

If life should have taught me anything, it's to pause before embarking on certain conversational paths, to give just a second's thought during such exchanges. It's unfortunate that inebriation prevents this.

'You spoilt little shit,' I say. 'Look at you.'

'At me?'

'Seventeen and already it's clear you'll amount to nothing.'

'Well, I had a good role model. The best, in fact.'

'You shouldn't be so harsh on your mother.'

'Ha, ha.'

'She can't help coming from a long line of fuck-ups.'

'You're a joke, Dad.'

I consider my son's face: the trendy erratic stubble, the

disdain for the man in front of him. I search for a wounding retort, but nothing other than a long guttural belch leaves my mouth.

'I'll move in with Mum when I get back.'

Again I know this is best left now. Further destruction will be regretted tomorrow. But I can't help myself.

'Shall I tell you something about your perfect mother?'

'I don't have time for this. Go back to your stories.'

'I'll give you a story, Jack. One of my best, this one. Starts just after your sister was born.'

Jack continues packing.

'Your mother had just gone back to work. We were both exhausted, struggling to pay the bills without help from her family, who were still disgusted by her choice of husband. Your sister would cry half the day and most of the night, as if being born was some form of torture. Four months of this and our nerves were frayed, occasional sleep was found in a bottle of pills. Then things just started to turn a corner, the worst over, when we found out she was pregnant with you.'

Jack stops packing and looks up at me.

'We couldn't believe it. B came home from work one day and said she wasn't keeping it. You. That it was too much to go through again. We argued for days, but I lost. She made the appointment and that was that.'

He frowns, as if my story has the potential to be hurtful yet makes no sense. I have his attention. I have an audience.

'What, you want to know what happened?'

He shrugs shoulders.

'Your sister's birth had been complicated. They said your mother wouldn't be able to have any more children. Hence, you weren't planned. Further tests showed she was just lucky getting pregnant again. Or unlucky, depending how you view it. There would be no more chances. It was then or never. It was you or no more. You see, she didn't want you. Given the choice . . . You were forced upon us. How do you like that twist?'

My son's face is blanched as he processes the words.

'So when you go running off to live with your mother, remember it was me who wanted you, not her. She'd have had you flushed away.'

He holds my stare for several seconds, hatred pulsating from his eyes, before pushing past me out the door.

Sobriety takes a small foothold and I know I've gone too far. Even for me.

'Jack . . .'

I run after him, grabbing his arm at the top of the stairs.

'Sorry,' I say. 'It's the drink talking. I was in character. It's not all true.'

He shakes free and I can feel the fury in him. I can't let him go like this. I fling both arms around him, lower than intended so that it resembles a rugby tackle. The momentum launches us down the stairs and for one ridiculous moment father and son are flying through the air cartoon-like. We take a few hits before landing heavily, having turned in flight, so that Jack is on top.

Pain emits from several regions, but I think I'm okay. Jack slowly clambers off of me, pulling himself upright with the banister. I'm relieved he seems free of major injury. My head throbs, from hitting it or the gin, I can't tell.

'Look at you,' he says once orientated. Some of the hatred has gone, maybe just for now, and his eyes start to well up.

'I'm sorry, Jack,' I say, but he's stumbling along the hall, wiping a bloody nose on his sleeve.

They were just words, I want to say. Sticks and stones

. . . Just sounds. They can't hurt you. They're not real things. They don't exist.

By the time I manage to call out that it's just a story, he's already slammed shut the front door.

Reload

THE SCROLLING ELECTRONIC display says the seat is unavailable from Taunton. I look along the carriage as people politely clatter into one another and decide to take my chances here; people, however selfish, rarely ask the old to move. Placing my tan suitcase in the space provided, I sit next to the window. From a plastic bag I take a small packed lunch, a flask of Earl Grey and a gardening magazine, arranging them on my quarter of the table. I have a collection of short stories that claims to be Chekhovian, but it's hard to give fiction the attention it deserves once you've resolved to take people's lives from them.

Tickets from Plymouth.

My trousers stretch over a wallet full of notes—a few weeks' pension plus some savings—which should cover accommodation, food, money for taxis and a handgun. A 9mm Browning will suffice, but I'll take what I can get.

Some of them have changed their names, moved around in the last ten years, but there's a website—www.justiceforcarl.com—that updates such attempts to slip from public attention. Sometimes photographs are uploaded, snapshots of seemingly ordinary people going about their business. None of them are legitimately employed. Some have children.

The young blonde woman opposite me hasn't looked up from her laptop since we left the city. There's a man to our right, perusing a fashionable paperback that boasts its sales beneath an ostentatious title. Every now and then he looks forlornly out the window, before dolefully turning another page. I wonder if he's troubled by love or loss. Trains do that, bring nostalgia or anguish spewing to the surface like emotional magma. (My melancholy started when steam became diesel. Still, they took my driving licence away years ago and asking for a lift would have invited inquiry.)

I suppose this final journey could be termed *a calling*, though from who or what, I'm not sure. Perhaps justice finds its own way in the end. It's never too late, as they say, to put the record straight.

I don't seek infamy—though I appreciate it will be hard to avoid in this age of ubiquitous *schadenfreude*. They'll probably base some reality TV show around my adventure, which would have made Mary chuckle.

Tickets from Totnes.

As our carriages are whipped through the Devon countryside, I look out of the window at the verdant hills that I have spent most of my life among, their pastoral innocence the antithesis of today's destination. I notice the blonde woman lifts her head out of the computer to glance at the emerald landscape, and I wonder whether it affects her at all, or if she's merely resting her eyes from a demanding cursor.

'We're lucky to have that on our doorstep,' I venture. She looks perturbed, as if I am breaking some assumed travel code about not talking to others.

'Oh, I don't live here. Just down on business.' She forces a smile and her eyes fall away at the end of the sentence, which I take to be the end of the conversation. And as if to confirm this, she casually taps a few keys. She is part of the generation that either distrusts strangers or just can't be bothered with them. I want to tell her how her indifference is in some small way connected to Carl, to him being forgotten, but it'll just confirm her view of senile old men.

My thoughts turn again to the men, that day outside the court over a decade ago, the crowd's disbelief, the fury that too quickly died down. Everyone knew something had gone wrong, that the script had been corrupted, re-written by some mischievous young playwright bent on avant-gardism. Twists of plot are all well and good, but there has to be a pay-off; you can't change the rules. They just let them go.

I see again their faces that day as they swaggered through their guard of dishonour: sneering, chests out, shoulders back. One stopped to light a cigarette, the gesture of a free man. I'd wanted him to take his sunglasses off so our eyes could meet. He took a long drag before blowing tendrils of smoke skyward, as if claiming the air as his own. At that moment, we became a mob. Yelling. Spitting. Some threw eggs; futile missiles, missing their targets as most missiles do, the ochrous yolk running instead down the black silhouette of interlocked police uniforms. Some of the younger ones tried to break the line and were in court themselves the next day.

And then off they sped, guilt known but unproven, leaving us only officials to shout at and our own impotency to ponder.

Tickets from Taunton.

A man with a briefcase sits next to the blonde woman. 'Do you know if the buffet car is open?' he asks. As he disappears through the swishing door, counting change, the pungent smell of stale coffee finds my nostrils. I can feel the burn starting to shoot up and down my leg, so decide to walk along the carriage. A young girl with vermillion acne and metal in her nose is making the Taunton man's drink. He smiles in recognition, asks if I'm okay.

'Need to stretch the old bones,' I say. We walk back, ungainly serpentine as the carriages bounce, past the toilet that only the brave and desperate use. Sitting down, I can tell the blonde woman is aware of how good the man's drink smells, but is either unwilling to pack up her lap-top or trust us not to steal it. Funny the people fate forces you to spend time with.

I consider my family: a son in his third marriage; a daughter you wouldn't choose. Their reaction to this plays out in my head. *Told you he'd lost it since Mum died. We should have gone round more. When did he learn to use a gun?* When? Long before they were born, in truth. But it's easy to make holes in bits of card with concentric circles on them. Just a game then, like at the fair. I was one of the best at that; could join all the holes up from a hundred yards with a rifle. No good at the real thing, though, when the time came. No stomach for it, they said. A disgrace. A coward. Go home and work in the factories with the women. No fucking use here.

A few of us stood outside the court that day, but then what? We all drifted back to benign lives, our families and gardens, television on Saturday night, checking lottery tickets, telling ourselves we held the moral high ground because we protested about some black kid getting stabbed. Some wrote to MPs, others started websites like the one I told you about. But what did any of it achieve? Carl was still dead. They were still free.

Tickets from Westbury.

I wonder if I'll be regarded a serial killer and how they decide. I think it's something to do with the gap between the first and the last, which in my case will depend on how quickly I find them all, rather than any perennial murderous impulse. I'd prefer the label 'vigilante', but will gladly leave that to others.

The pain pulses through me. I wince and rub my leg.

'Arthritis?' the Taunton man asks.

I nod; it invites fewer questions. He beams at his correct diagnosis. He's an acupuncturist in London, returning from an alternative medicine conference. Says I should go and see him. Gives me a card.

I'm endeared by his enthusiasm for Chinese remedies and their philosophy to the point where I resist challenging him on the bastardisation of words like 'energy' by his kind. He talks of blocked *meridians* and *chi*, how stress is going to be the epidemic of the twenty-first century (which I suppose is fortunate for him), and of the need to breathe properly. Our breath is supposed to come from our *dan tien* or somewhere. Says he'll have me right in six sessions.

We flash through a tunnel.

'What about homeopathy?' I say.

'Sorry . . . ?'

'Do you believe in it?'

'It's not really my field, but it seems to work.'

'But its principles are flawed. How can a drop of something be stronger in a swimming pool than in a glass of water? That's what they say, isn't it? The more you dilute it, the more potent it becomes. How can water retain the memory of something once it's gone?'

'Well, I . . .'

'There's no evidence beyond anecdote.'

'Much of medicine is still a mystery. There's so much we don't know.'

'Exactly. So why are people allowed to make such promises?'

There's a pause unique to strangers. We avert our gazes to the window, a chance to reload.

I want to ask him about reiki. About iridology, reflexology, aromatherapy and all the other things Mary used to waste money on. But the longer the rhythmic vibrations of the train fill the silence, the more soporific I become and the fight goes out of me.

Tickets from . . .

Mary, sit down. There's something I want to tell you. No, don't be scared, it's nothing like that. Just listen. I was young, eighteen, cocky little so and so. Jack the lad. Nothing new there, you say. Been the best at everything in school. Friend to everyone. Life and soul, as they say. Just had no direction, though. Tried an office, but it wasn't for me. Worked in the docks for a month, then an abattoir, then on the trains. I kept looking without knowing what for. So I signed up to fight fascism. The training was tough, but I felt so alive. We were sent to Africa where the sun was white and seared through your uniform like acid. We still played football like mad dogs at midday. Even tried to play in a sandstorm. And then my war started. The Australians were chasing the Italians along the coast and we set up in Beda Fomm to stop their retreat. Just sat there in the bloody desert waiting for twenty thousand men to come over the horizon. We were outnumbered ten to one, but held them off. They threw everything our way for two days. Some of their tanks broke through our lines, but our field guns took care of them. We reached one, flame and thick black smoke billowing out of her. Three men lay dying in the sand, arms and legs scattered about like a cartoon. In a final act of defiance, one of them started to draw his pistol, but his wounds made it near impossible. I raised my rifle, shouted something, looked him in the eyes, but still he tried to get his gun. 'Shoot him, Stephen. Do 'im.' I lined up for a head shot. He just grinned, his teeth blood-stained. I knew I was supposed to shoot him, that it was an order, that it was him or me. There was a shot, and a warm sensation in my leg. Yes, my bad leg. All I could see was his manic eyes and bloody smile as Sid emptied into him. I was sent home a week later.

I must have fallen asleep for half an hour or so, because in the distance, dreamlike, I hear someone saying we are ten minutes from Paddington. I am disoriented, my brain trying to catch up, pain firing up and down my leg like electricity.

The Taunton man smiles warmly. 'Out like a light,' he says.

The station throbs with the fug of diesel. Hundreds of people scuttle like ants, anxious to make a connection. I walk until the pain eases and find myself outside. The November air bites into my cheeks; a miasma of breath forms on each exhalation. My thoughts return to the five men; men oblivious to war; men who owe their freedom to an absence of evidence.

This is where it begins. My second chance. I reflect on a line from some novel: *My bones ache with all the lives I am not living*. For the first time in ages, my bones did not ache.

Team Build

I THOUGHT ALL THIS team building went out in the nineties. Back then it seemed every other month I'd break a nail trying to build a dry stone wall in the name of camaraderie. Once the pricks in charge became convinced it increased productivity and profit, there was a bottomless pit of cash for managers to drag their team up Snowdon in the rain or throw them off some cliff dangling on a rope. Nobody complained—for most people planting an arboretum on Dartmoor or crawling through mud in some pothole was preferable to showing the great unwashed around badly-decorated semis in Bracknell.

I've moved up from that now. Deal in the luxury end of the market—barn conversions, period properties, nothing less than half a million. But even I can't hit my targets, let alone a performance bonus, building a bloody raft out of palettes and barrels. Christ knows the margins are tight enough these days. It was fine when everyone was a property developer, watching those programmes with the pouting presenters who can hammer a wall through and still look dressed for cocktails, as they tell everyone to move up the ladder. Business was, as they say, booming. You only had to show up for your two percent. Didn't matter what the place looked like when you were armed with words like *potential* and *portfolio*. People only saw what you described to them. *Imagine opening it all up*, I'd say, *unearth the house's true essence. Create a space that says who you are. Then sell it to the person on the rung below.* Everybody was doing it. There seemed no end.

But then the doom mongers started muttering about recession, the credit crunch, unsustainable prices. A Crash. Talk about a self-fulfilling prophecy. Now nobody's buying or selling, no one's lending; it's a renter's market, which means belt tightening all round.

If I told you the repayments on the Beemer, you'd blush. Everything's going up: petrol, bubbly, facials. Foie gras's rocketed. These are tough times for everyone. If I don't get Employee of the Month soon, Jason says we might have to start renting out the cottage in St Ives for the winter. The thought of having the world and his wife using our Harrods cutlery and sleeping in the four-poster turns my stomach.

So you can imagine my reaction when management announced this trip was compulsory. No doctors' notes, no crying off last minute. It's only two days, they said. Bring us all together. Harmonise our energies.

I've already counted thirteen bruises on my legs alone from the paint-balling yesterday. It was the most ridiculous sight imaginable as we clambered over tree trunks in camouflaged overalls and helmets that flattened your hair for the rest of the day, trying to capture and defend territory. It was like one of those wars you read about in the Sunday supplements. Wasn't a total waste of time, though. Just after lunch I got Caroline from close range plum on her size twelve behind (too many oysters, not enough hours in the gym). She made a noise like a cat being run over.

'Sorry,' I said, 'sensitive triggers, aren't they?'

'We're on the same team.'

Same team! There are no teams in this business. At least she can't sell anything this weekend, either. She's nine points behind me, but has been for the last few months, only to offload a five-bed in the suburbs an hour before deadline. I swear she's fucking the boss. I mean, we all have, at some time, but coming from behind to win four times in a row takes the piss. On top of the bonus, she's had a skiing weekend in the Pyrenees, dinner for two at Gordon's new place and audience tickets for *Deal or No Deal*. I'll just have to try harder.

The lodge we stayed in last night was barely fit for savages. Not a free-standing bath or heated towel rail in sight. I was too exhausted to stand in the utterly-lacking-in-power shower, so just collapsed on one of the slabs that passed for beds. And you'd think we deserved a proper breakfast after all that. Some smoked salmon and Philly on a cinnamon bagel. A hot latte. Oh no. There was a vat of what looked like gruel and some stewed tea in plastic cups that I wouldn't serve to our cleaner. There was no alternative on offer, so I shut my eyes and pretended Nigella had knocked it up.

Today's canoes are Canadian kayaks apparently, you know, the ones that man on TV knocks up in twenty seconds out of a box of matches and some twine. Craig must have picked up on the tension between Caroline and me yesterday, as he's deemed it beneficial for us to share a cockpit down river. Caroline makes a joke about using me as a paddle, which only a few people find funny. I try to think of a witty retort about her bringing more make-up with her than anyone could use in a lifetime, but Craig blows the whistle on his life jacket and we're off, ten of us climbing into five canoes with the dexterity of newly-born giraffes. I make sure I get in the back of ours; I can't have Caroline's fat face staring at the back of my neck (when you've been under the knife, angles are important).

The water is a gentle ripple, but we're told it gets whiter further down. Most of us drift downstream sideways on, or facing the wrong way. Paddles clash or get stuck in the riverbed, some falling in and floating down ahead of us. I'm no rower, but Caroline has the coordination of a drunk.

'You're working against me,' I say, but she's too busy trying not to lose face with the men, whom she thinks adore her and whom she didn't see all laughing when we found her failed application for *The Apprentice*. Priceless. Can you imagine Sir Alan putting up with her for more than a minute? She didn't even make the second round, it seems. I mean, if you don't want people to know these things, don't use your work email. I didn't.

'You're fired,' the men giggle to themselves and an oblivious Caroline gushes at the attention.

They all know I'm better than her at the job. She thinks her NVQs count for more than the two grand I've spent on neuro-linguistic programming seminars this year. (Dr Rob taught us that to master our destiny we must first master our minds, so every hour I say my meta-mantra: *Nothing-has-any-power-over-me-other-than-that-which-I-give-it-through-my-conscious-thoughts.*) Jason said it was money better spent on a timeshare or hot tub, but you have to invest in yourself, in your potential, if you want success. You are your own best asset; it's win-win when you think about it.

We finally get the canoe pointing in the right direction and lead the way down the river. We'd been told to look out for herons and kingfishers, but if there was any wildlife, our arrival has scared it away. I've never understood people who go on about nature, choosing to stay in a tent, walking for the sake of it. (Don't get me wrong, I can lie on the beach with the best of them. When there was that health furore with sun beds, Jason and I flew to Tenerife four times in one year to top up.) But why be outdoors when it's cold or wet? That's what nature programmes are for. And as for living out here, all those smells from farms, miles from a decent restaurant or salon. I read last week that people live here because they find it less stressful. What could be more traumatic than spending half your life reversing up roads because someone forgot they needed to fit two cars on them? It's here they need a congestion charge.

Not that we live in the city, you understand, that would be too terrible for words. You need a balance, as my life coach says.

Two of the men, Greg and Rich, have found some rhythm and speed past us looking smug. They're still wet behind the ears, poor things. Ordered Merlot at the annual dinner last month, bless, which had me and Jason in fits. They flick more water than they need to into our path and I give them the finger.

'Come on,' says Caroline. 'Let's race them.' She slaps the water with her paddle, getting me wetter still. There are a few cheers from behind as we take up the challenge and pursue the men. Within a couple of minutes we've rounded two bends and left the others behind. The men, seeing us catch up, have put their backs into it and pull away. As the river narrows it starts to froth and flow faster, meaning we have to paddle less for speed but more for direction, as small rocks sit up in our way.

After a few minutes a fallen tree is blocking almost half the river and I can see the men glancing back in anticipation of some entertainment.

'We need to get across to the other side,' I say.

'You're the one who's supposed to be steering.'

As she tries to put in some big strokes, her paddle

merely skims across the top of the water and hits me hard in the side of the head.

'Fucking hell!' I scream. 'You stupid bitch.'

'You've got a helmet on. Stop moaning. Come on, they're getting away.'

We manage to miss the tree, although its top branches whip us as we pass. There are actual waves now bumping us about and I can feel the porridge slopping around inside me. Every time Caroline paddles I get a face full of water and I can only imagine how dry my skin will be after this.

'Paddle the opposite side to me,' shouts Caroline, but it's all I can do to not drop mine in the water. Through the spray I can just make out the men, who seem even further away. The waves form a whirlpool and as we hit it our canoe lunges to the right and I'm sure we'll both fall out, which they definitely didn't tell us might happen. Then we're flung to the left just as far before the front dips and I fall forwards crashing into Caroline's back.

'Let go of me,' I hear and realise my arms are wrapped tightly around her waist, which is thinner than it looks but could still do with a few sessions of lipo.

'Grab your fucking paddle,' she says, which I see is still on the floor. The front of the canoe suddenly bucks up, sending me back to my half, although facing the wrong way. As the whirlpool spits us out, I can just make out one or two walkers on the riverbank, though it's impossible to tell if they look shocked or disgusted.

I manage to turn around and sit up, grabbing my paddle and we're off again, Caroline shrieking that we need to go faster. We soon spot another tree lying across most of the river and there seems no way we can miss it this time.

'We need to get to the bank,' I say.

'We can go under it.'

I look for the men, to see if they made it, but there's no sign of them, just white waves spitting upwards.

'When I say *duck*,' Caroline says, 'duck.'

I'm about to protest, but my open mouth fills with water and I just splutter and choke; I'd cry if it wouldn't give the bitch as much pleasure as a sale. The rapids take us towards the trunk and I can see there's a gap beneath that tapers to nothing where it meets the water. Caroline looks back at me, her eyes intense and excited.

'Under there,' she says, pointing to where the tree is highest.

I start paddling hard but this just turns the boat sideways.

'No, you stupid . . .'

Caroline tries to correct it, but it's too late as we shoot towards the tree. She forgets about shouting *duck* and crouches down as much as she can as her end of the canoe heads straight for the trunk. There's a thud and a yelp from her and this time we do capsize. The water takes all my breath and my head goes numb. Everything turns black and silent. I panic, trying to work out which way is up. Feeling around, I find two legs kicking out and I use Caroline's body to pull myself to the surface. I stand upright and realise it's only a few feet deep. The canoe is on its side, wedged under the trunk. I tell a flapping Caroline that she can stand up. I'm exhausted and shivering.

'My arm,' she shouts above the torrent and I see that it's stuck between a thick branch and a rock. 'Get me out.'

I glance up and down the riverbanks to see if we're alone. One of the oars is still in the canoe, so I grab it and start to force the blade between her arm and the branch.

'What are you doing?'

'This might hurt a bit,' I say.

'No, wait, it'll . . .'

I jump up as much as I can and let my entire eight-stone frame push down on the oar. Another scream, this time much lower in pitch. The branch moves an inch or so and Caroline pulls her arm out.

'There,' I say.

I feel myself being dragged onto the bank by several sets of arms. Craig's voice is saying something about us going too far, missing the rendezvous point. Someone unclips my helmet and tries to take it off.

'Mind the hair!' I shout, for a moment forgetting it's been submerged.

I'm aware of Caroline being put next to me, yelling in pain as she's placed down. 'I think my arm's broken,' she says. 'She broke my fucking arm.'

'At least you're alive,' Craig says.

Lying in this hideous place, I take some comfort from the thought I'll soon be heading home. To civilisation. To a hairdryer.

'Looks like you'll be off work for a while,' I say to Caroline.

'I can't be. I can't.'

Really, I think, as my breathing slows, it's all about the winning for some people.

Extracts of Love

IN ANY MAMMALIAN social group, particularly the higher order ones, there will exist a member more acute to fluctuations in light, sound and movement. Such traits are innate and benefit the group, as the member acts as an early warning system to imminent threats. These members are lighter sleepers and tend to have faster reaction times. With such heightened sensitivity, however, comes behaviour detrimental to the member, such as a neurotic manner, a greater susceptibility to illness, and the tendency to fall deeply in love.

To: Robert James
From: John Bradshaw, Head of Human Resources
Date: 5.6.2007
Subject: Attendance Management

Robert,

It has been brought to my attention that you took three days' sick leave last month, all of which were Wednesdays. May I remind you that the company's policy on unacceptable absence can be read using the following link: http://dynamicsystems.co.uk/hr/attendance

No formal disciplinary action will be taken in this

instance, but you should consider this a warning that further absence will be viewed seriously.

John Bradshaw

To: Sally Barnes
From: John Bradshaw, Head of Human Resources
Date: 5.06.2007
Subject: Attendance Management

Sally,

It has been brought to my attention that you took two days' sick leave last month, both of which were Wednesdays. May I remind you that the company's policy on such absence can be read using the following link: http://dynamicsystems.co.uk/hr/attendance

No formal disciplinary action will be taken in this instance, but you should consider this a warning that further absence will be viewed seriously.

John Bradshaw

To: Sally Barnes
From: Robert James
Date: 5.06.2007
Subject: ???!

What happened to you on Wednesday? I waited for ages. God I hate all this sneaking about. Am getting lots of flack here so may have to change our arrangement. When will you tell David about us? I hate pushing you but I can't stand this waiting. I do love you, but I guess you know that. Sarah took it as expected—I've been on the settee ever since ☹ I know we agreed to wait but I just couldn't any longer. I know this is right . . .do u feel it too? There's no going back. Need to see you, touch you. What were those things you did to me the other afternoon? Are they legal? x

To: Sally Barnes
From: Robert James
Date: 6.06.2007
Subject: ☺

Can't concentrate on work—would rather count the hours till next we meet. Sarah has seen a solicitor. Talk about not wasting time. I suppose I should do the same, fight my corner, but all I care about is seeing your sweet face. I make it 149 hours since I was inside you. And counting. Did you like the pottery? It's raku. It reminded me of our day in Cornwall. Just think, every day can be like that soon. I feel 18 again; stomach's like a tumble dryer. Not sure if I'll get any of the house, but who cares if we're poor? We can keep animals and live off the land.

Reckon the kids will take it badly. They can come visit once we're settled. I know they'll love you.

What do you think of Barcelona? Always wanted to go—just a long weekend. We could explore all day—I have a guide on Gaudi.

Better go, am getting accusing glares from all. Hope David isn't awkward. xx

To: Sally Barnes

From: Robert James
Date: 7.06.2007
Subject: Where are you?

Did you get my messages? I hope you're not sick, my sweet one. Perhaps your email's down. Will find an excuse to come to your wing later. I hate this pretending.

Sarah's saying I'll be lucky to see the kids at all. I suppose this should make me sad, but as long as I've got you . . .

Where are you? I hope you weren't teased about the flowers.

To: Sally Barnes
From: Robert James
Date: 8.06.2007
Subject: ☹

Came by your office but you had company. Felt like barging in anyway, telling them love is more important than some corporate orgy in Manchester. God, I hate this place. Someone asked why I'd removed Sarah's picture from my desk, whether everything was okay. Sniffing for gossip rather than genuine concern. Just didn't want her bloody face accusing me all day as well as all night. The girls are still here, by my plant—their love unconditional, I hope. They'll understand when they're older. How I'd love to put your picture on my desk; might set tongues a waggin. I expect David looks lovingly out at you. Even that makes me squirm with jealousy. I even hate his two dimensional image having claim to you. Gotta keep up appearances, I suppose.

Divorce seems such a dirty word.

Perhaps we can meet another day if Wednesdays are difficult for now. Let me know what you think. I'm aching all over for you. xx Where are you?

To: Sally Barnes
From: Robert James
Date: 9.06.2007
Subject: Fuck her

Sarah has thrown me out. Bitch. Says I should go live with you. If only. I'm staying at Paul's, but his wife's asides imply this is strictly a transient arrangement. Will go 'home' to see the girls two afternoons a week. Never thought I'd be one of those dads. I guess it'll be easier for you without children—just David to appease. Tell me you've told him. Tell me everything is going to be okay. Tell me this love can beat everything thrown its way.

Got caught sketching your face on my pad today. Major tuts all round. Just cos I'm not a cynical old bastard yet.

Sarah asked where we do it, so I told her. What's the point lying now? Said she'd never forgive me for bringing you into her home. I said it was my home too. She said didn't twenty three years count for anything. She called my a cunt. I've never heard her use that word.

Just realised I have odd socks on.

To: Sally Barnes
From: Robert James
Date: 10.06.2007
Subject:

Sarah took a load of pills last night. They say she'll be okay. Bit of organ damage at worst. The girls have gone to her mum's, who says the two afternoons a week thing is not practical as she lives too far away. Down to phone calls now. Not that the kids are really speaking to me anymore. Think they're told to take the calls. They're too young to know about love, else they'd see.

When you leave David, I thought we could rent somewhere. I know we haven't talked about it, but why wait? Neither of us is getting younger. I'll pop into the agents after work, get some details. Will need a bedroom for the girls. Do you prefer traditional or modern?

This ironing lark is impossible. Look like I buy my clothes from Oxfam. Getting some looks re my beard. Forgot to pack a razor. Must get to the shops later. Do you like facial hair on your men?!!

To: Sally Barnes
From: Robert James
Date: 13.06.2007
Subject:

Paul's wife says I can stay a week but no more. She heard about Sarah and the pills. God, they weren't even friends. Paul does what he's told, though, so looks like I'll be homeless. Thought of going back home as no one's there, but I think the locks were changed.

Hope things are easier your end . . .

I love you.

To: Sally Barnes
From: Robert James

Date: 13.06.2007
Subject:

Where the hell are you . . . ?

To: Sally Barnes
From: Robert James
Date: 14.06.2007
Subject:

That new temp just gave me a look. Smelt the whiskey I reckon. Nosy bitch.

Can't say I've done any work all week. We might need to live on your income for a bit at this rate!!! Just kidding. I think.

To: Sally Barnes
From: Robert James
Date: 14.06.2007
Subject:

HELLO?

To: Sally Barnes
From: Robert James
Date: 14.06.2007
Subject:

Your phone has been diverted for a week now.

To: Stephen O'Connor, Managing Director
From: Dick Travis, Head of IT
Date: 12.06.07
Subject: Misuse of email

Steve

A security sift found 27 emails sent from Robert James to Sally Barnes last week. I can see no business need for this volume, so am retrieving their content to forward to you later today. Also, James' hard drive contained some sort of diary, an extract of which follows.

Let me know how far back you wish me to check his mail.

Best
Dick

Extract found on Robert James' C Drive:

24/5—Yesterday is still with me. I keep it fresh while my senses allow. Breathing in, eyes closed, I get her fug of smoke. She has just lit up her post-coital Marlboro Light, drives me fucking mad. Not the smoking—seem to reserve the puritan in me for the kids. It's the sense of omnipotence her eyes exude the second she exhales, capturing every subservient man's essence, every man who was ever a slave to beauty. She has me, knows it, lets me know she fucking knows it. I had tried to shift the dynamic, assert an ersatz confidence, pretended I could take or leave it, but she sees through me as if I were a lovesick jellyfish.

And men can't leave it. Not ones like me, anyway. I tell myself we have a spiritual connection, a cultural and aesthetic one as well as a corporeal one, but who the fuck am I fooling?

I mean her skirt yesterday, bohemian and long, instead of proving asexual, merely drew attention to the air between her legs. I sat behind her on the hotel bed, trying to breathe it in, wishing that gorging myself on the body in front of me wasn't the only thing that now mattered in my life.

I console myself that history is littered with men who've thrown away their wholesome lives in the wanton pursuit of a dangerous woman. Ha—just looked up and found Johnson staring at me, somehow knowing my typing isn't work. Like he's ever fucked a real woman. God, what a prick. Women go for men like him cos they'll never be lured away.

But who says we're designed to stay with one person forever? Not the scientists, anyway. Only the idiots who gaze skyward for moral regulation, and most of them are overflowing with guilt.

Well, not me. I'm taking my second chance. Love will follow on from lust for her. We can't turn back now. It's all or nothing . . .

To: Robert James
From: Stephen O'Connor, Managing Director
Date: 12.06.2007
Subject: Disciplinary meeting

Robert

Our IT department has brought to my attention your misuse of the company's electronic media, specifically using the internal email system for social ends and keeping a diary during work hours.

You are formally invited to attend an interview in my office at 11:00am on 15th June 2007 to discuss what action will be taken. You are strongly advised to bring a union representative with you if you have one.

Stephen O'Connor

To: Robert James
From: Sally Barnes
Date: 13.06.2007
Subject: Not goodbye . . .but au revoir!

I'm sorry I haven't replied for so long. Been a bit chaotic my end. I've thought hard about this and there's just no way I can do this to David—it would kill him. I only ever thought of what we had as fun—at least it used to be. I never meant to give you the wrong impression. I hope we can still be friends and that it's not too late to sort things out with Sarah.

Take good care,
Sx

To: Fred Dale, Head of Security
From: Stephen O'Connor, Managing Director
Date: 14.06.2007
Subject: Robert James

Fred,

The company's Head of Marketing, Robert James, has

been sacked today, following a violent outburst this morning. He's been sent home and has to clear his desk by midday tomorrow. Please escort him from the building in the normal way.

Stephen

To: Stephen O'Connor, Managing Director
From: John Bradshaw, Head of Human Resources
Date: 22.06.2007
Subject: Employee Death

Stephen,

Just to let you know I have arranged for some flowers to be sent to Sally Barnes's funeral. Did you want to sign the card? Rumours are they needed dental records to identify her!

The police want to come in this week to discuss Robert James, who is now in custody. Is morning or afternoon better?

John

The Arrival

NONE US REALLY remembered where he came from. Just rode into town on his Vespa one day, charmed the pants off everyone with his stories and ideas. We usually took months checking someone out, setting little initiations, looking for a past. But the arrival of Jesse Powell seemed to suspend the rules.

I liked him because he could get into any house or safe in under a minute. Mortise locks, deadbolts, timers—there hadn't been a lock invented that could defeat him. Never really worked out how he did it; his little secret, he'd say. Alarm systems, too, were there to overcome, to outwit. And once inside a place, he'd ghost about as if walking on air.

Some of the guys protested at first, aired reluctance at this character who appeared more hippy than criminal mastermind—but he soon became all things to all people. Some, who just a week earlier spat feathers as they uttered his name, could be heard heaping praise: Jesse this, Jesse that. Even when the weird stuff started happening (watches not working, mobiles ringing in the night for no reason), no one wanted to blame him. His talents, and therefore worth, blinded us all.

For a gang we were large, twelve if you included drivers and muscle, though we only went into properties in twos. Run like a business, we possessed a corporate nature that served us well. We were hardly the Mafia, but it's really only amateurs who get caught. The hierarchy was designed to encourage fierce loyalty. You had to be able to trust the person next to you as if they were family; betrayal is all the harder when you love or respect someone.

You started at the bottom like an apprentice, worked your way up with hard graft and by doing what you were told. If you showed promise, you'd gradually be exposed to the more lucrative work. Yet within weeks, Jesse was making some of the big calls, telling us what jobs to go for, that we should have Sundays off. At meetings we used to argue deep into the night, locking horns over detail, but Jesse would just stand up, sweep his long fringe behind an ear, and everyone would listen, hanging on every gently-spoken word as if hypnotised. I couldn't claim to be any different, least not at the start.

He got us to target ever-grander properties and businesses.

'Why risk going down for a fake Rolex and some laptops?' he'd say.

And so we spread operations out into the Downs and the Cotswolds, concentrated more on stately homes, where we acquired antiques, sculptures, artwork. (Thought we had ourselves a Leonardo once, but it turned out to be fake.) We had to learn to identify what was valuable and how to offload it.

The richer the client, the more security they enveloped themselves in, but this was hardly an issue with Harry fucking Houdini in your team. Jesse started turning us from well organised but small-time crooks into relievers of the super-rich. Thievery almost felt righteous. If anyone ever questioned him, challenged his methods, he'd fix them with those penetrating eyes, telling them to have faith. We were, he said, simply redistributing wealth.

I went out a lot with him in the beginning.

'Do you play chess?' he asked me once as we surveyed a large house on a fifty-acre estate. We were squat in a corner of this garden maze, freezing under a cloudless sky, staring up at the windows waiting for the lord of the manor to finish banging his lady.

'Used to. A little.'

'Carved my own set once,' he said. 'Out of redbud.' He looked at me as if this should have meant something.

'Red . . . ?'

'Redbud. It's a tree.'

'Bit of a whittler, then?'

'I dabble. Old man was a carpenter. Come on, let's have a game, pass the time.'

'What? How?'

'In our heads. I'll have white: e4.'

Desperate not to lose face, I tried to visualise the board. For a few moves I kept up, but was soon lost.

'Er, knight d4?' I said.

'We playing the version where you can have more than one piece on a square?'

'Fuck this.'

'Come on, I'll spot you a rook if you like.'

'What's the point if I can't remember where mine is?'

That's what he did—endeared himself, yet reminded you of his superiority. Other times he'd show a more caring side, which unnerved some of us. Coming back from a job on the moors one night, we hit a fox.

'Stop the van,' Jesse said.

Phil was driving and thought he was messing about.

'Stop,' he said again, still calmly but with intent.

'Fucking thing's dead, anyway, speed we hit it.'

I could just make out Jesse in the side mirror as he walked through the exhaust smoke, tinged red from the rear lights, and bent over the creature. After a minute or so, just as Phil was suggesting we leave him there, I saw the animal leap up and scurry away through the hedge.

'What?' he said, as we drove away. 'We're all God's creatures.'

Over the next few days, the incident was retold amongst us, but as soon as we wondered whether he was going soft, we were reminded of an occasional reckless nature, which tended to reveal itself after the wine had been free-flowing. Once, after a particularly profitable week, we were partying hard—few lines, got some of the girls over. Thom had this airgun and we set up some targets in the garden, shot at them through the lounge window. The room soon reeked with testosterone; bets were made, notes still flecked with grade A were won and lost. Mary was flying as usual, always two or three hits ahead of everyone; more flesh on display than a footballer's wife. Groupie, follower, I don't know what you'd call her. She loved to flirt with bad boys—nothing more to my knowledge—rubbing up against them as they took aim. Jesse hadn't met her before and for once seemed the recipient of a spell.

'What about you, new boy?' said Mary. 'You a good shot?'

He announced that the rest of us were mere boys and that he could hit a bull's-eye through his hand if he wanted, which everyone doubted, especially Thom, who knew the gun.

'Go on, then,' she said. 'Be the big man.'

So Jesse picked up the weapon, extended his left arm and placed the end of the barrel against the centre of his palm. Closing one eye and resting his arm on the sill, he pulled the trigger. The gun, though, was nowhere near powerful enough to make an exit wound, and after the snap, a steady trickle of blood flowed from the entry hole down his wrist. We all just stood there watching as Mary took his hand and held the puncture to her mouth until the bleeding ceased.

'Fucking idiot,' I said. 'Come on, let's get that seen to.'

'Nearly there,' the nurse said, trying to find the two-two pellet with a scalpel, clearly wondering whether the police should be called.

After ten minutes of poking and prodding, she gave up. 'Whatever was in there, it's gone now.'

He didn't, as they say, get the girl that night. But Mary came around eventually. They always did with Jesse.

The good times rolled on; the bizarre stuff continued, but no one cared. The word *retirement* was tossed about. Some of us had started seeking more legitimate enterprises, investing in property abroad. One or two more big jobs then go our separate ways. But Jesse seemed to have a different agenda. He started suggesting we give away some of the money. *For good luck*, he said. *For karma*.

'You been watching too much fucking Robin Hood,' said John.

'Do what you like with your share,' said Thom.

So he did. And in ever eccentric ways. Donations to charity were anonymous, but then he started riding into towns, seeking out someone with a cardboard box for a home and dropping a bundle of fifties in their lap. I mean, you just can't do that and not draw attention to yourself, even if you keep your helmet on. Word got about. The papers wanted to know the identity of this mysterious benefactor of the poor, what his motives were, where his money came from. He started to become a minor celebrity, albeit a nameless and faceless one. Beggars started appearing everywhere, praying they'd be in the right place at the right time. A reward for information about him was offered, which was a bit rich. They named him the Motorcycle Messiah. A documentary was made following the homeless as they went on spending sprees courtesy of their saviour. The authorities despised him.

We firmly suggested to Jesse that he stop, but he just said there was nothing else to spend the money on, that there was only so much one person needed.

I called a meeting without him. Something had to be done—he was jeopardizing it all. Trouble was, he knew everything, he'd been in on all the big jobs for months, knew all our contacts and outlets. He could put us all away for a decade or more unless we had a serious clean up.

It took about two weeks. Tracks were covered, anything that could link us to Jesse was destroyed. Multiple alibis were constructed; work suspended. He was suspicious, I'm sure, but most of his attention was taken up giving his money away or getting high with Mary. We met again to discuss an exit strategy, the details of which were left to me.

I hate barbeques. How the smoke finds me wherever I stand; how the food is either raw or cremated; the way most men think they look good in shorts and sandals. I especially hate hosting them, but we needed a window of an hour or two.

'You seem on edge,' said Jesse as he sliced a bread roll for me and filled it with charred meat and onions.

'Lot on my mind,' I said. 'Some big decisions to make.'

'Oh, I'm sure you've made the right ones.'

I tried to brush off his sarcasm, but his composure was more unsettling than ever today. Everyone else was either awkwardly silent or showed exaggerated affection towards him.

'Glass of red?' Jesse asked me.

'Why not.'

As I took it from him, he held on for just a second so our hands touched.

'A toast . . .' he said.

'To what?'

'To friendship. All friends together.'

We clinked glasses.

'All friends together,' I said.

'If you haven't got friends . . .'

' . . .what have you got?' I finished.

He looked around at everyone, beaming like some proud father. 'I wish you'd think again about helping other people.'

'Been over this, Jesse. Go and work for a fucking charity if that's what you want.'

'I just wouldn't want you to forget about it.'

My phone rang. As I took the call, Jesse's eyes seared into me. All done, the voice said and I hung up.

'Got to make some calls,' I said. 'See you in a bit.' I walked around the house to the front garden, making sure I could see him through the windows. I forced any guilt from my mind and dialled.

'No, I don't want to leave my name. No, I don't want to say how I know him. Number 35, yes. Church Street. In the loft, behind the water tank.'

They'd find two suitcases. One stuffed to bursting with bags of Columbia's finest, the other with dirty money and an untraceable Uzi for good measure. Should be a ten stretch, at least.

Did I feel bad? Honour among thieves and all that? Maybe a little. I had become fond of him—we all had.

He'd been good for us, but he was a loose cannon now. His time had come. You have to do the right thing.

I had one more call to make. Hate talking to journalists, but I can't stand to see a reward go uncollected. A kiss and tell story, I think they call it.

I walked back through the house. Jesse had left the barbeque and was wandering around the garden. I took the sim from the back of the phone and tossed it on the charcoal before going to find him.

'Finished your calls?' he said.

'All done.'

'Good. I'm glad.'

The Little Man

DAD IS DOING his thing with the dark, telling us to hold our hands in front of our faces, asking if we can see them, which we can't. We sit still—me, my sister Katie and our classmate—the only sound the *drip drip* of mineral-rich water falling from stalactites, echoing around the pitch black chamber. We've heard this, me and my sister, so many times, but it's for Clare's benefit.

We'd asked her in school one day, in the alley they all smoked in.

'Well, if you're scared . . .' my sister said.

'Of what?'

'Bats,' I said. 'Spiders.'

'Shut up.'

'Go on, Clare, go with the freaks,' one of them said.

Freaks was the most benign of their judgments, but probably the most accurate. Mum used to say God moved in a mysterious way and had made us special for a reason, though she never said what it might be. She used to come caving with us when Sophie, our little sister, was alive, but now she stays at home with the curtains drawn, listening to the same audio novel over and over. We go into her room for an hour after tea each day. She lies there contemplating the ceiling while we tell her about school.

We give up trying to see our hands and turn our lights back on. The chamber is vast. Dad once told us you could fit all the people in Devon in here if you packed them tightly enough, but when me and Katie did the calculations, there was nowhere near enough room, however much you squashed them in.

We look in a crystal pool. Dad shines his light into the water and tells Clare about the blind fish. He says how they evolved without eyes, how they use touch to navigate.

'What do they eat?' she says.

I tell her that nutrients get washed in from above ground, but she only wants Dad to tell her—Dad who produces freaks but isn't one himself. Katie and I ignore her and look for another pool we know.

'Not too far, you two,' Dad says.

Sometimes there are shrimps. Their skin is see-through, so you can see all their organs, like in an X-ray. There aren't any today, which I know makes Katie sad. I squeeze her hand and we go back to the others.

We clamber between the giant boulders that fell here millions of years ago and squeeze into a small passage. Dad leads and I go at the back because I've done more caving than Katie. Clare goes in front of me and every time she gets a bit stuck and panics, she kicks me in the face.

After a while we get to my favourite place in this cave. You crawl along for ages thinking it's just cold mud and rock, and then it appears from nowhere. We sit down and Dad tells us to turn our lights out again and begins.

'Hundreds of years ago, there lived an evil squire called John Cabell, who was said to have sold his soul to the Devil. On the 5th July 1677 he died and the terrorized villagers buried him in a stone crypt. On the night of his internment, a phantom pack of hounds came off the moor to howl at his tomb.'

I can sense both Clare's fear and Katie's excitement. Dad continues.

'On each anniversary of his death his ghost was seen leading the shrieking hounds across Dartmoor. To stop his soul escaping, the villagers placed a slab on the tomb and built a wall around it. But still there were reports of a strange red light glowing from behind the iron bars. The evil squire now had only one escape route, tunnelling into the ground. But when he finally got into the cave system below, he got stuck between two rocks, where he remains forever.'

Dad turns his light on and the beam shines right on the Little Man. He's about six inches tall and is where a stalagmite joined with a stalactite. It should be white but is grubby where cavers have touched it over the years. You can see two arms, a body, a face with ears and a nose and a large hat, like a squire's. Dad sometimes brings a little mirror, climbs across to it, because he's allowed to, and places it behind so you can see why it's called the Little Man and not the Little Woman, but he doesn't today, probably because he doesn't want Clare to see its penis.

I swear I could stay down here all day because it's so beautiful. Once, when Mum and Dad had been shouting at each other all holiday, Katie and I slipped away from the main group and just climbed around on our own, looking at all the red and orange fins and white straws. We got a bit lost but weren't scared. Dad was so cross, he just kept crying and shaking me, saying how we could wander around down here for weeks and not be found, which was fine with us.

Sophie was the youngest and Mum's favourite. Doctors had said there was a reasonable chance the curse would skip her, so it was a shock when she turned out to be the most disfigured of us all. It was as if Mum decided she needed more love as a result. The night before Sophie started primary school, Katie and I heard someone crying, so we snuck downstairs. Dad was comforting Mum. We heard him say that science would one day be able to help us all, make us normal. Back upstairs, Katie said she wouldn't want to change anything about herself, anyway, and I agreed.

We leave the Little Man and head back. We're about half way to the chamber, in a bit of the passage you can stand up in, when Clare gets stuck again. Not because it's too tight, but there's a ledge we have to walk along and a little drop to the side that I know is only a few feet, but she thinks is really deep. I tell her to use the ridge on the wall to pull herself along, but I can see she's scared. She just stays there, looking into the wall, like she's on the edge at the top of a skyscraper.

'You okay back there?' says Dad, who's ahead round the corner.

'We're fine,' says my sister. 'Here, Clare, take my hand.'

Clare reaches out and starts to move along the ledge. Katie looks at me and I nod. Just as Clare goes to take my sister's hand, Katie withdraws it. As Clare falls away from the wall, she grabs at a stalactite above her, and it looks for a minute as if it'll hold her, but even though it's been there for thousands of years, it snaps clean in two and falls with Clare into the hole. There's a thump when she hits the bottom. I stare up at the stump, which looks just like a broken bone. Years ago, on one trip here, I caught my helmet on the bottom of a small fin and broke the tip off. Dad just told me to be more careful, but I knew he was really angry with me all summer. And that was no big deal, but I know this stalactite is one of the most important in the cave, because apart from the Little Man, it's the one on all the postcards. And now it's broken.

Clare is crying out like she's been shot. Dad comes back along the passage and shines his light down on her. He asks her if she's okay, if she can move, but I know really we're all looking at the long piece of white rock next to her. She says her leg hurts and when Dad tries to pull her up, she screams so loud it hurts my ears because there's nowhere else for the sound to go. He says she might have broken her leg and that they'll need to stretcher her out, which makes her cry more. Dad climbs down and uses his belt to tie her broken leg to her other one.

Dad wants me to stay with her while he and Katie get help. He says our batteries should last, but just to be safe, to turn one off and wait till they come back. As they crawl away, my sister looks back at me and smiles.

It was so much harder for Sophie once she got to secondary school. My sister and I had each other; we shared several lessons and would always meet up in between the ones we didn't. We tried to hang around with her, but it seemed to draw more attention.

The thing I love about caves, as well as how dark and wet they are, is how quiet it is, and it's ages before we can't hear Dad and Katie crawling away in the distance. And then it's just us. I try to talk to Clare, but she just snivels.

'You shouldn't have grabbed that,' I say. 'It's probably been there for nearly a million years,' which is an exaggeration.

'It was your fault. You were making me go too fast.'

Just then my light shines on a spider on the wall next to her head, sat there with its eggs, which look like little balls of cotton wool. Clare sees it and starts all the screaming again, trying to crawl away from it. She's shouting to me to pull her out and when I don't she takes her helmet off and starts hitting the wall like she's hammering a nail.

'Stop it,' I say. 'You mustn't do that.' But the next hit makes a squelch and when she pulls the helmet away there's just a black mark on the wall and another one on her helmet.

We just sit there for a minute not saying anything.

'I can't stay here,' she says. 'Get me out.'

I think for a minute: 'You'll have to crawl through that gap at the back. It loops round and comes back out here, but it's tight. I did it one year.'

Dad found Sophie gently swaying from a joist in the garage. I know this because Mum went looking for him and her screams brought us in. We all just stood there silently watching Mum trying to get her down.

Extracts of Sophie's diary were read out at the inquest, cataloguing months of misery. She got it worse than me or Katie ever did. Nobody was named, just references to the leader: an older girl called C.

Clare looks at the dead spider again and then at me and then starts to fumble around, pulling herself along with her arms like one of those people with no legs. She finds the spot I mean. She starts to climb through it, but half way in she gets stuck because her battery pack won't fit through as well.

'You'll have to take it off. Pass it back to me. When you're through I'll come round from the other side and pass it through.'

'How can I see where I'm going?' she says.

'I'll shine my light along the tunnel from up here.'

She thinks about this for ages, then unbuckles her belt,

unclips her lamp from her helmet and passes them back to me. I shine my light so she can see along the passage and she pulls herself along, crying out every time her bad leg touches the floor.

'Keep going,' I say. 'I'll come round and meet you the other side.' She takes ages and I can hear her snivelling all the way.

I look again at the spider's eggs and wonder if any of them will hatch. I read that it's usually about half and that only half of those survive because the baby spiders, which are called spiderlings, eat each other to survive.

I take Clare's lamp and battery pack and drop them in a hole I know that no one else does, and I hear them fall for a second or two before they reach the bottom. I start to make my way back to the main chamber, where there are some helectites I want to draw in my book later. As I crawl further away, Sophie's beautiful face pops into my head. A scene from a camping holiday, the three of us running around a cornfield, smiling and laughing, hiding from each other, while Mum and Dad put the tents up.

I hear Clare shout my name a few times, but after a while I can't hear anything. I think she's found one of the deep drops along that tunnel and is probably stuck between the rock, just like the Little Man.

Acknowledgements

To Ranald MacDonald, who suggested great things were still possible.

To all the teaching staff on the creative writing MA at the University of Plymouth, especially Hayden Gabriel, who suggested I write some stories.

To my parents, all six of them.

To James Walkley-Cox, for his encouragement and friendship.

And to Alison Smith, who changed everything.

Thank you.

'The Last Supper' was first published in *Brand* (2008); 'The Method' first appeared in *Riptide* (2008); 'Seeing Anyone?' won the *HappenStance* Short Story Competition (2008); 'Breathe' featured as a podcast on the website *Fiction Flash* (2008); 'Old Enough' was published in *Cadenza* (2007); an earlier version of 'Reload' appeared in *Words* magazine (2003); an earlier version of 'Staring at the Sun' appeared in *INK* magazine (2005) and 'Busy. Come. Wait.' was first published in the *Willesden Herald New Short Stories* 4.